I Can't Stand Losing

by the same author

Stories about Cricklepit Combined School

THE TURBULENT TERM OF TYKE TILER
(Awarded the Library Association's Carnegie Medal)
GOWIE CORBY PLAYS CHICKEN
CHARLIE LEWIS PLAYS FOR TIME
(Runner-up for the Whitbread Award)
JUNIPER: A mystery

JASON BODGER AND THE PRIORY GHOST
MR MAGUS IS WAITING FOR YOU
NO PLACE LIKE
DOG DAYS AND CAT NAPS
THE CLOCK TOWER GHOST
THE WELL
THE PRIME OF TAMWORTH PIG
TAMWORTH PIG SAVES THE TREES
TAMWORTH PIG AND THE LITTER
CHRISTMAS WITH TAMWORTH PIG

Edited by Gene Kemp

DUCKS AND DRAGONS
Poems for children

ff

GENE KEMP

I Can't Stand Losing

faber and faber

LONDON · BOSTON

First published in 1987
by Faber and Faber
3 Queen Square London WC1N 3AU

Typeset by Goodfellow & Egan Ltd Cambridge
Printed in Great Britain by
Richard Clay Ltd Bungay Suffolk

British Library Cataloguing in Publication Data

Kemp, Gene
I can't stand losing.
I. Title
823'.914 [J]   PZ7
ISBN 0-571-14773-9

for Chris Kloet
and for Margaret Turner, with grateful thanks

Characters

Chapter One

The female body is my hobby so when I happened to spot my mate Wally out with this girl, Lynne, I jumped about a bit because all of a sudden I felt that life was about to take on a whole new meaning, boyo, and Lord knows I needed a lift just then.

"You didn't tell me, you two-faced son of a . . ." I thought to myself as Wally dragged her round a corner out of sight, out of my sight, quick as Jack Flash, though not quick enough for me to miss that she had a face like a peach melba, a face to launch a thousand nuclear missiles, and a figure with more ins and outs than the coastlines of Scotland, or Norway maybe, does it matter, you get the picture. But speedy as he was for old slow-off-the-mark Wally, I'd spotted her, and it was all too late. For him and for her, for both of them. I'd put her straight on my hit list. Tough, Wally boy, tough.

I didn't know then, of course, that her name was Lynne. It was only later that I'd lie back in bed playing word games.

> "I'd like to sin
> With Lynne.
> For she's not thin, that Lynne.
> Oh, how I'll grin
> The day that I win
> With Lynne . . ."

And so on. You get the idea. My old English teacher would've been pleased. Once he said I'd got about as much idea of poetry as a sack of cement, which goes to show that school doesn't bring out the best in people. There I lay in a blue haze of smoke and love on my bed going through the alphabet finding all the words that rhymed with Lynne, though "bin" didn't do a lot for me or her. But as I said, that was later.

At the time there was Wally the wally, disappearing round a corner dragging this chick, this honey girl, this may-blossom after him in case she encountered yours truly in all his splendour, me, Moi, Patrick Gates, entrepreneur extraordinary, millionaire in the making, lock up your daughters, mister, and your girl-friends, wives, and sisters, beware, take care if Patrick's there. And spotting Wally and friend on the run, I felt that life, a bit draggy lately*, had just once more opened up before me beaming and waving on a blue, blue horizon.

"Here I come, little unknown person," I sang and got going.

It took me two days to bridge the gap between seeing that girl whipped round a corner, surprise, surprise writ all over her delectable pan, and sitting beside her on a park bench with puffly, frothy blossom cascading all around and framing her. That small and perfectly formed nose was wrinkling a bit, out of curiosity or like a bunny rabbit scenting danger.

Quite right, too. If she knew anything at all about Patrick Gates, she'd know there was danger.

But I knew about her. No, I'm not revealing my

* My ex-girl-friend Anna was giving me hell, as I was trying to get rid of her and that's never easy.

2

sources of information, my devious contacts, why should I? The network's good. I've worked hard on it so why give it away? But I'm telling you, in no time at all I'd got her name (Lynne Persephone Martin, she'd always hated the middle name but now she sometimes used it) and telephone number. Daddy an executive in an electronics firm, Lynne Persephone his only child, no scrubber this one. Doing A Levels in Modern Languages, howzzabout that? Bright they said, with the right accent, and best of all the lovely smell of money all about her, all the goodies, cars and jacuzzis, antiques, computers, stereos, videos, the high tech. game, swimming pools, patio, large secluded gardens, used to riding but losing interest, rabble-free holidays abroad off-season, a cottage in the country, talk of a flat in town (London to the proles), colour supplement living . . . all Patrick Gates ever wanted, Moi, Patrick Gates, Number One Whizz Kid.

So what was a girl like that doing with a berk like Wally? And him not breathing a word about her.

Wally, my mate Walter Byack, has been my friend for many years, while I've stuck up for him more times than you've had hot dinners. I've had to for he's always been wet. So I reckon he owes me. And I'd share my last tin of Coke with him as the earth blew up and we all went together though in such circumstances I'd rather head for the whisky and leave the Coke for Wally. What you've got to admit is that his name is so right for him, typecasting from the start. Sometimes I've wondered if his parents were round the twist, and they are, or what's left of them as his dad walked out one evening muttering about a can of dog meat and was never seen again.

He didn't even take the dog with him but then that's life, says Wally's mum. She didn't seem to mind.

That uptown girl can only be going out with Wally because, being new here, she doesn't know anyone else. Which means she wouldn't know about me and what they say about me, good.

And there she sat beside me on that bench in the park.

"Call me Patrick," I murmured soft and low, looking at her in a way I know works, at least it always has ever since I was thirteen and took out Tracey Brewer, sixteen and big with it. She taught me a thing or two or even a hundred, which came in useful as I pursued my hobby.

Remember when you were a kid at school? And what is your hobby, Patrick Gates, answer me, boy, you must have a hobby? We had all manner, fishing, swimming, football, collecting, always collecting, stamps, butterflies, fossils . . . Wally was really dead keen on fossils. That time, on the school trip, up on those blue soggy cliffs, blue lias they called them, a funny name, and I shouted Wally Boyo, there's something absolutely brill there and lowered him into a deep cleft, then I walked away with all his fossils and he couldn't get out, and he was sweating and crying until old Grouty at the other end of the beach remembered him, so I ran and rescued him.

"You're rotten, Patrick," he blubbered all over his little face. "I don't know why I'm your friend, 'cos you're so rotten," and he wouldn't sit by me on the coach back home, his mug streaked with crying.

Even then I knew crying's a waste of time, 'cos life's a giggle, a marionette operated by Sod's Law. They gave me a house point for the best fossil collection.

Wally soon came round, though. He needed me. Now I can't help giggling inside as I sit on a park bench with this bird in the spring sunshine and he doesn't know, the wally.

"Patrick," Lynne said, with a sort of break in her voice. "Why did you ask me to meet you here?"

"I told you on the phone."

"You said you had something to tell me about Walter."

Ah, Walter to her, was he? I suppose he'd have to be. He wouldn't want her to think of him as a Wally. Her voice was deep and broke every now and then as if she hadn't learnt to manage it properly. And you could sweep the road with her eyelashes. The other bits and pieces looked all right, too.

"Yes, I have. Thank you for coming."

"I only came because you said you were his friend. I don't normally meet people I don't know in parks. It could be dangerous."

"Not with me. You're safe with me." I tried to look as if I was the most complete opposite ever of the Yorkshire Ripper. And I am. Females are for loving in my book. The smile I gave her was so wide and gentle, it nearly met round the back of my neck.

"About Walter, then. What about Walter. You say he's your best friend but he's never mentioned you."

"He wouldn't, I think. That's all part of it."

"Part of what? What are you talking about? Or rather, not talking about?"

"How long have you known Wally? Walter, I mean."

"About three weeks, though I don't know that it's any of your business."

"That explains it then," I murmured very seriously.

"Explains what?" She looked lovely, all pink and cross.

5

"No full moon during that time."

"What do you mean, no full moon? Are you nutty or something?" She stood up. "I'm going. I haven't time to sit here listening to rubbish."

I stood up too, very politely, for the old slob routine was not going to work with this one.

"Please listen. If you care about him, that is. Don't go. It is important, really."

She sat down again. So did I and put on a serious face.

"How did you come to meet him?"

"At a friend's party. It doesn't matter and it's nothing to do with you, in any case."

Huh, I thought, it is something to do with me if there are parties going on with Wally invited and not me. Something would have to be done. For if I'd gone to that party, I'd have met Lynne there and Wally wouldn't have stood an earthly. Not that he would now, by the time I'd finished.

"Look," I said, dropping my voice really low. "I can't really tell you anything because it's not my place to tell you. I only wanted to warn you to be careful. Oh, not against old Wally, he's a saint, a lamb . . . only watch out for full moons . . ."

"You mean he's a werewolf or something . . ." She looked amazed and interested. That wouldn't do. He'd got to be nutty and boring, not crazy and fascinating.

"No, I can't tell you. But it's harmless really, only I wanted to warn you to be careful as you seem a very nice girl. I'm glad, very, very glad you're going out with Wally. He's always seemed to be the other way, you know."

"The other way?" she cried.

6

"Look, I have to go now. But I'll see you around . . ."

"Wait a minute . . ."

"Must dash. Any worries – just ring me. I'll come in an instant if you need me. Bye now. Gosh, you're really beautiful. Lucky Wally."

I moved away at speed. Leaving her standing there, looking lost.

"Oh, don't worry about his legs," I cried as I went through the park gates. "Bye, Lynne."

"His legs?" I heard her cry, and "What's wrong with his legs?" followed me as I ran down the road.

Whistling I made my way home. Only a question of time now. She'd be ill at ease with Wally. She'd want to ask about legs and full moons. Wally's always ill at ease anyway. They'd soon fall apart and who would be there to pick up the pieces and comfort them both? Why, their friend and yours, Patrick Gates. More whistling.

"How's old Squeaky Gates, then?" asked a voice behind me, a voice I didn't like, always putting the mockers on, Soupy Lethbridge catching me on her ten-foot-long legs, Robin Hood boots, ten-foot-long ear-rings, a wartime flying jacket and the cheek of the devil.

"Get lost," I returned, hurrying it up. "Sex object."

Her legs were longer than mine. She caught up with me.

"Turned you down, did she?"

"Little you know," I snarled. Soupy Lethbridge after Lynne was like HP sauce after strawberries and cream. Common as muck is Soupy Lethbridge. I shot over to the other side of the road and hurried on home.

Chapter Two

"You'll be all right," my mum said. "You'll manage." Then she kissed Dad on his nearly bald head, Zebedee on his almost totally bald head, grinned at me and walked out of our house, and out of our lives.

I didn't know *then* when I came in that this was a day to remember, the day that divided the men from the boys.

At the time I just headed for our all-in living, eating, sitting, lounging, cooking, quarrelling room, hoping that all the grub hadn't been swiped by my ever-loving family for I was starving.

And there they were in mid-nosh.

You've seen those films with people seated on elegant chairs at polished tables, everywhere gleaming with glasses and silver, candles and roses in bowls and all that jazz, well, if that's what turns you on, don't come to 17 Constance Place. And don't ask me who Constance was as I don't think I can bear to know.

Don't come here for gracious living. We shan't be featured in *Homes and Gardens*. We have no swimming pool, no jacuzzi, no gym, no sauna. Our bathroom looks like a reject from an overcrowded gaol and don't hold your head up high when you walk through a storm here or you'll get drenched from the guttering.

8

The unsecluded gardens are open regularly to the public ever since the wall blew down and created the largest litter bin in town. All the neighbouring moggies and various mangy man's best friends have taken out a second mortgage with us as they love it here. The patio consists of a heap of bricks, two old broken drainpipes and a thrown-out washing machine. The balding lawn backs on to the public incinerator, but we don't charge for viewing.

Come right in and meet my folks as they chomp away merrily. Take Gramps, oh yes, please take Gramps. As far away as possible. All those phoney stories about lovable old eccentrics whose warm and meaningful relationships with the young ones is the best thing in all their lives, well that's not Gramps and me. No. Gramps has turned me into a keen supporter of EXIT, the euthanasia society. If I had any kind of money I'd donate it cheerfully. Recently I've worked out that to be the kind of wise, kind old geezer they rabbit on about you've gotter start early before the mould sets for good (or bad), and Gramps didn't stand an earthly as he was obviously a five-star, four-letter-word bloke from early nappies onward.

Gramps was getting to grips with his specially mashed and sanitized nosh, his false teeth rising and surging out of the mush as he masticated or failed to masticate for some had wedged between his gums and his free-floating National Healths. My mother was fishing out bits and pieces for him. Mostly when this happens you look away, only sometimes it holds you captured like a horror film, as you wait to see just how gruesome it can get. It's strange really, you read in the paper about old people being mugged. The

9

only time *anyone tried mugging Gramps* he coshed the mugger so hard with his walking stick he was hospitalized for a week.

The seedy-looking guy rummaging in the sideboard in an agitated manner is my Uncle Arnold who writes for the local rag. Now Uncle Arnold is a thrown-out man, thrown out of more pubs, clubs, betting shops, etc, than you've had hot dinners. Finally, unable to stand him any longer, Aunt Edna threw him out as well. Two years ago. So where did he turn to? You may well guess. He's been here ever since. Not that he's noshing. Whisky is all the body needs, he says.

I headed for the kitchen and heaped up my plate, looking at the unlovely gathering to see if there was a space, no, so I carried my plate to the sideboard where Uncle Arnold eyed me with suspicion.

And meet Zebedee, nine months old or so, splattering his plate with podgy glee, mashed spinach and rice flying through the air, gurgle, gurgle, splodge, splodge, little face abeam, big shiny head likewise, no hair. He was perched on Mum's other side while she tried to spoon food (mush again) into him, but he had other ideas so most of it was finishing up in one ear.

Then meet the rest.

On the piano stands a framed photo of us horrible bunch of little kiddie-winkies, yuk. I've thrown it away twice but each time somebody rescued it, and brought it out again. Nat – the eldest – she's got her arms round Mike, cherub with golden curls (whatever happened to him?), then me with no front teeth, Chell, and Pip Emma, an afterthought we all regret, though she's not as bad as Mike, no one could be as bad as Mike. It's amazing the effort he puts into being universally unpleasant. He devotes such care and attention to it that it would almost be easier to get a job. And there we all are smiling and Pip Emma lying on a cushion on the carpet. All five of us.

"Why the crowd?" I asked Mum once.

"Inefficiency," she replied.

"More like criminal carelessness," I said, moving at speed to avoid the backhander she dealt out.

Uncle Arnold was still muttering into the sideboard.

"Have you got it?" he hissed at me.

"What?" I inquired through what was either lamb casserole or Lancashire hotpot, I wasn't sure which.

"Me whisky. Somebody's had me whisky. Is it you?"

"No. It'll be Mike."

"Hey, Michael. Leave my whisky alone, will you . . . ?"

"I never touched it, you stupid old fool," Mike snarled. The cherub grew up into a nasty of very uncertain temper, depending on whether he's high or manic at the time. Occasionally when he's neither, he's laid back, very.*

*As he was now laid back on the sofa with his girl-friend Loopy, Soupy's sister. Don't ask me how that pair got those awful names. It's like Constance Place, I'd rather not know. She's not at all like Soupy, in fact she's not like anything except a shaft of dust, a bony blonde with a lined face at eighteen and no hope. You'd have to have no hope to have Mike as a boy-friend.

"Well, someone's had it. Someone in this house," Uncle Arnold muttered.

"Oh, belt up," I said. "You sound like an Agatha Christie inquiry."

"What a place. No organization. No whisky Nothing."

"Git on your bike then," shouted Mike.

"Find something else," I said. "We don't want you here. I never had your rotten whisky."

Uncle Arnold muttered his way up the stairs.

"Gone to his secret hiding-place," put in Pip Emma, beansprout hanging out of her mouth. She's into vegetarianism.

Gramps was sniggering into his mush, causing a flurry.

"Can't he be fed somewhere else?" I asked Mum who got up, came back with clean cloths and tidied up both Gramps and Zebedee.

"Gramps took it. That's why he's laughing. I saw him carrying a bottle up the stairs." Pip Emma knows everything, I'm sorry to say.

"I put one over on Arnold. Never liked the chap," giggled Gramps into his mush which surged and heaved along with him.

Natalie, Zebedee's mother and my sister, was making her face up at a mirror. She doesn't like meal-times. She doesn't like participating in things she says, including marriage. She won't even speak to Zebedee's father let alone marry him.

"You going out?" asked Dad.

"Yah."

"Who's minding the baby then?"

"Mum."

"Again?"

12

"She likes it. Don't you, Mum?"

"That baby won't recognize you if you meet it out," growled Dad. Mum didn't answer. She and Zebedee were wrestling with a bottle, though she reached out from time to time to help Gramps come to terms with his teeth. Dad sighed heavily. Ever since he was made redundant, he's taken to sitting in his chair and sighing all the time and he likes Mum to stay near him while he does this.

I looked at them all through Lynne's eyes and pushed my plate away. They gave me bellyache. You can see everything's hopeless, there's no light at the end of the tunnel, which goes uphill all the way to where there's no gold at the foot of the rainbow because there's no rainbow.

What was I doing here with this crowd of has-beens and no-hopers? Moi, Patrick Gates, wanted out.

"Cheerio," I said and headed for the door. I needn't have bothered for no one was listening but in the doorway I banged straight into Uncle Arnold.

"What a dreadful place this is. It's disgusting. I don't know why I stay here and put up with it. I can't find my whisky anywhere. It's really too bad. I shall stop it out of your money, Bessie."

"You never give me any," said my mother, "so it won't make any difference, you old misery. Gramps, tell him where you've hidden his whisky and stop messing about."

"Shan't," said Gramps petulantly.

"So you've got it! I'll settle you, you old rascal," cried Arnold, advancing on him, waving trembling hands in the air. Gramps stood up in instalments.

Mike leapt out of his sprawling position.

13

"Do us a favour," he yelled. "Come on, come on, come on, get at it and finish each other off, you stupid old geezers. I'll place odds on Gramps. He's older but more vicious."

My mother spoke calmly. "Michael, be quiet. Arnold, stop it. Gramps, sit down before you fall down. Pip, you know where the whisky is. Well, fetch it. And I don't want to hear another word about it all."

A kind of peace fell and once more I tried to get away, only this time my path was barred by sister Chell, surging and panting, wearing what looked like a silk scarf with a bra over the top and blue hair falling over one eye. Two combs and three bracelets fell off as she came in but that still left plenty.

Chell sees herself as the sex symbol of Constance Place. She's alone in this.

"Back upstairs and put something decent on," said Dad. Chell took no notice. No one ever takes any notice of Dad.

"Do what your father says, Michelle," said Mum.

"Rotten, you're all stinking rotten. Stinking rotten knickers," stormed Chell, but she stamped back upstairs, tearing off bits and pieces as she went.

"Here's your whisky, Arnold," stammered Pip, appearing from under the stairs. Arnold grabbed the whisky, Gramps started to mumble, the doorbell rang, so did the phone, and Dad called upon Death to release him soon from earthly strife.

Above all this rose Pip's voice, quite effortlessly. She can outshout a town crier. She's eight and Mum had her when she and everyone else thought she was past it, and now she's turned out to be either a gifted child or round the twist, depending on how you

14

think about it or her. She doesn't really care whether anyone listens or not, though she does like getting Mum's attention, which ain't easy in this house.

"Mum, they think the force, y'know the basic force of the universe, was split into four . . ."

"Go jump in a lake . . ."

"Stone the crows" (plus any other vulgar expressions).

"Stop showing off . . ."

"Belt up."

". . . gravity, electromagnetic, a weak and a strong force – I'm doing this for my project – and they've got this theory about it, y'see, but to prove it by experiment they'd have to make ever and ever such a huge, great, big bang that it would blow everything up . . ."

"And the silly fools will do just that if somebody doesn't stop them," interrupted Mum very loudly and clearly, whumph. We all shut up and gazed at her. She folded a tea-cloth and walked out of the room. And we waited. Not saying a word. I don't know why. I don't think anyone else knew why either. It was just her voice, the way she'd spoken.

At last she came in again. She was wearing very old trousers, wellies, a vast anorak of Dad's and carrying my rucksack, already packed . . . already packed . . .

"Cheerio, then," she smiled round the room. "I'll be in touch."

"But . . . what . . ."

"Oh, me, I'm off to Greenham," she said. "You heard what Pip said. Well . . ."

And it was then she said, "You'll be all right. You'll manage." She kissed Dad on his nearly bald head,

Zebedee on his almost totally bald head, grinned at me and walked out.

Her head poked back round the door and I thought, it's OK, OK, she's only joking. She used to be a joker, I remembered suddenly. When we were little. Before life got her. But she only looked at Dad and said, "You'll sort it out. So shall I." And was gone.

Dad sat there looking as if he couldn't sort five red beads from five blue beads.

Time dropped a fat silence packed with all manner of things into the middle of the room. Then pandemonium broke loose. The phone stopped ringing. The doorbell ringer just went away.

Chapter Three

Pip was first out after her, screaming,

"Mummmmmmmmmmmm don't go, you need me, you neeeeeeed MEEEEEE . . ."

"Hang on a minute," I yelled, coming up a close second.

"Mum, you can't get along without me," Pip shouted.

The taxi disappeared round the corner at the end of the road as the rest waited. Pip ran down the street crying –

"Let me come with you, then," but it had gone.

I ran for Dad's old banger, with him and Pip coming up behind. It was parked half-way down the road as we haven't got a garage. Dad fiddled with the keys.

"I'll drive," I said. (I was taking my test any day now.)

Dad took no notice but heaved himself into the driver's seat.

"Dad, I'm quicker!"

"You're a menace. Get in."

He fiddled with the seat belt for hours, then looked at me and said:

"Where d'you think?"

"The station, of course. Where else? She'll have to catch the London train and get off at Reading."

"Must be, I suppose." He sighed heavily and started the engine.

Soupy Lethbridge screeched to a halt on her beautiful Honda, why should she have a machine like that? But then she's got pots of lolly, having a Grade A job, is there no justice?

"Something wrong?"

"Mum's gone to Greenham. We're going after her," cried Pip from the back of the car.

"I know she wanted to. So she's finally made up her mind. Great!"

And Soupy roared away on her Honda leaving me so hopping mad that . . .

"What the hell does she know about it? And she could have given me a lift. We might have stood a chance of catching Mum."

Dad was crouched like a praying mantis over the steering wheel but absolutely nothing was happening except for Nat, Mike, Loopy and Chell arriving. I got out.

"Comeon, comeon, push, push . . ." I cried.

Somehow we pushed, then I leapt in as the ancient engine glugged into a kind of life. As we crawled our way through the rows of small terraced houses that line the way to the station, I said:

"Did you have a row, Dad? To trigger this off, I mean?"

"Oh no. We're just the same as we've been for years."

"Oh Lord. That explains it. No wonder she left."

"I don't know how she could leave me," came a voice from the back seat.

"Shut up. Get a move on, Dad. Can't we go any faster than thirty?"

"This is a built-up area, lad. Don't forget that."

I shan't forget this I thought as I refrained from head-banging on the car window.

"I bet the train's gone when we get there," said Pip.

"You haven't got any takers, kid."

The car, like Dad ever a reluctant mover, juddered gently to a halt just outside Wilf Passmore's garage.

"Comeoncomeoncomeoncomeon, Dad."

"It's jacked in. I can't budge it."

I was half-way out of it. "I'll run on."

"I'm coming with you," screeched Pip.

"You're not." And I went.

But the train had already gone, of course.

On the way back I collected Pip and we returned to the garage where Dad was haggling with old Wilf about hiring another car. After long negotiating he managed to get hold of a very, very old Ford of a type that Noah helped to build when he was taking time off from the Ark.

"What are we going to do then, lad?"

I told him the train had gone but if he wanted to drive to Greenham there and then I'd go with him.

"I don't know what to do, lad," he said, slowly shaking his head. I held my feet still in case I kicked him from here into the middle of next week. If you get to his age without knowing what to do there isn't much point in anything, is there? Might as well drop dead.

"Look, make up your mind, Dad."

"Well, it's like this, lad. I don't think we stand a lot of chance of finding her tonight, as it's a big place, like. At least, so I've 'eard. Oh, I wonder why she had to go running off like that? It's not like Bessie, Bessie's a good girl. She wouldn't leave her duties. Oh, I know she were a bit wild when she were young

19

– she allus says you teck afer 'er a bit . . ."

As he stood there blethering, his original northern accent came back stronger and stronger though he left his native town years ago.

". . . but she's a good girl, ar Bessie, she wouldn't let anybody down, would she?"

"Fetch her back NOW in this car. She can't manage without me, you know," said Pip.

"Well, there's Gramps and Arnold and the little girls and the baby to look after . . ."

"I'm one of the little girls and I WANT TO LOOK AFTER MY MUM. SHE DOESN'T KNOW WHAT SHE'S DOING," shouted Pip. For once I agreed with her. But it was no good.

"Without Bessie there, me first duty is to be home, announced Dad.

Even at his speed, maximum twenty-five miles per hour, we arrived eventually back at Maison Gates.

"Whatever are we to do?" Dad asked again as we went in, but I didn't bother to answer. For the beautiful people were waiting for us to have their ration of say.

"You didn't stop her, then?"

"That car's useless."

"What you doing now? You'll have to do something, Ronnie. You can't have her going off like that. What's she thinking of, I'd like to know?"

"Crazy, she is."

"Round the bend."

"She's been funny for weeks."

"It's her time of life. Women are like that."

"What a sexist remark . . ."

"It just happens to be true . . ."

"I knew something was up . . ."

20

"I don't know how we shall manage . . ."

"Oh, stuff that. It won't make any difference . . ."

"It will to me. Who's gonna look after Zebedee?"

"You try it, you're his mother, you layabout . . ."

"I do a job, don't I?"

"What about me? Bessie shouldn't have gone off and left me . . ."

"Oh, you'll be all right, Gramps. Don't worry . . ."

"You're bound to worry at my age . . ."

"Well, if you ask me . . ."

"Who's asking you?"

"If you ask me, it's disgustin'. The whole thing's disgustin'. Bunch of lesbians, all on drugs, sleeping in wigwams . . ."

"It's not like that . . ."

"Whatever it's like, it's agin the law. So it's not right. I don't hold with . . ."

Pip was crying. She tugged at my sleeve.

"She won't go to prison, will she?"

"Course not. Not Mum. They wouldn't dare."

"Where's Zebedee?"

A wail from aloft told us where Zebedee was.

"I took him up but didn't settle him," said Nat.

"I can hear that."

Pip cried, "I want Mum to put me to bed. I always read her a story, you see . . ."

Chell was having hysterics and tearing her clothes off on the stairs.

"Look," I shouted to Pip. "Dad'll give you fifty p if you belt up and get that raving lunatic sister of yours upstairs and read her a story instead. OK?"

Pip turned off the tears just like that. I thought she would.

"OK. But make it sixty."

"Done."

Pip led away the sobbing Chell.

"And now, dear sister Natalie, if you don't settle your own screaming brat up aloft I'm going to wring your neck so honest I am," I said.

But Nat's tough.

"Dad'll do it," she shrugged. "I've got a date. With a *real* man, not junkies, juveniles and has-beens. So cheers. I'll be back, later. Oh, and if anyone has any ideas about me taking Mum's place till she gets back here, forget 'em. I don't intend spending my life on other people, thank you."

"Dad," I began, but then what the hell?

"I'll be back later," I said and followed Nat.

Chapter Four

And there waiting for me at the end of the road was Anna, yeah, Anna, the last girl-friend, Super-glue Anna, sticks tighter than anything. I turned to go back the other way, but she ran and grabbed me.

"I've got to talk to you, Patrick," she said, in a desperate voice. She was wearing her yearning look and enough make-up for an Apache brave about to go on a war dance, which in a way she was doing, as I knew from the look in her eyes, moo-cow eyes, she fixed on me as she breathed heavily.

I wanted to run, but where could I run to?

"We've been through all that, Anna . . ."

"No, I want to talk to you. Properly . . ."

"We did that before, at least I don't think I used any wrong words . . ."

"Stop making feeble jokes, that's your trouble, you're always making feeble jokes . . ."

"I wish it was, then I wouldn't have many problems as most of my jokes are pretty good really. Sorry, but I do have to go, Anna. Tim's waiting for me . . ."

"Let him wait. And you're probably seeing some girl, you liar. Listen, you two-timing Casanova, no one on the face of this planet is gonna pick me up and drop me just like that . . ."

"Anna, Anna. Listen to me. Nobody has dropped you. We had a mutual agreement that when it was all over then we'd part friends and there'd be no ill feelings."

"I've never been so humiliated, Patrick Gates."

"Why, whatever's happened, Anna? You'd better tell me about it. As a friend I may be able to offer some advice."

"Stuff your advice. And your rotten friendship. After what you said about me to Don Parker . . ."

"What did I say about you to Don Parker? I don't remember."

"You said you'd had the first course and were full up and sick of it, so he could have the pudding to follow."

"And you believed I'd say a thing like that? Oh, Anna . . ."

"Yes."

"Who told you this load of rubbish?"

"His sister Deborah told me. So there. What have you got to say, Patrick Gates?"

"Nothing. What is there for me to say? Except I've never said anything like that about a girl, especially you, Anna, in the whole of my life. And wait till I encounter Deborah Parker and her rotten brother. I'll deal with them. She's only jealous of you, y'know."

"Oh, you could tell me why."

"Well, I wouldn't take her out, though she practically went on her bended knees. And then, you're so much prettier. I mean, you're one of the loveliest most smashing girls I've ever laid eyes on in the whole of my life, absolutely fab you are, and I'm just sorry it didn't work out that's all. But then, that's life. I guessed you'd be after bigger fish than me. Natural, really."

"Oh, Patrick, look, let's go to the old place and have a really good natter, huh?"

"It's very difficult, right now, Anna, believe me. Nothing I'd like better but . . ."

"You're sick of me."

Too true, too true, I thought, funny how you can go off people. I'd been crazy about Anna for three weeks or so and now – well, never wanted to see her again ever, or even sooner. Given a straight choice I'd just as soon go out with Loopy. All females were rubbish when I thought of Lynne, my Lynne, my Lynette, my rainbird, my sweety, my dream girl . . .

Out loud I said, "We've got trouble at home." I lowered my voice in a desperate and serious manner. "I can't tell you. I can't tell anyone. But Dad's nearly going crazy. And he needs me, Anna, he really needs me and when my Dad needs me, Ly . . . Anna, then I'm there at his side."

Bring on the violins, that's all we need, I thought, but it was going down well. Nearly slipped up with the names though. Have to watch that . . .

Her voice changed, went softer.

"Patrick, I didn't know. Can I help?"

"There's nothing anyone can do. I just have to see it through. All these problems . . . and then, my exams . . ."

I'd overdone it, I knew in a minute.

Her voice hardened.

"What exams? You never take an exam. You've made a point all your life of not taking exams."

I made my face brave and suffering.

"I don't like talking about my affairs, Anna."

"We all know why that is. You've got so many there isn't time."

"Anna, we're getting nowhere. Look, believe me, I just can't get out much at the moment, but it's nothing to do with you . . ."

"You've got another girl . . ."

"No, I haven't," I answered, fingers crossed. "And when you said, Anna, you wanted out, I agreed though it hurt, it hurt deep inside, but I said to myself, Patrick, I said, if that's the way Anna wants it that's the way it's gonna be, no matter . . ."

"Listen, you you gonk, you pig, it was YOU FINISHED WITH ME!"

"Don't shout, Anna. I don't want you to feel guilty. A girl must do what she's gotter do even if it means hurting others."

"Y-y-y-you . . ."

"Look, you're not making a lot of sense, Anna. Go home and have a nice rest and I'll give you a bell tomorrow, huh? Will that do?"

I was edging away but she jumped and grabbed me again, if I wasn't careful, I'd get eaten alive in the street, for Anna is a big, strong girl, not little like Lynne . . . I wanted to cry for help.

And help was on the way for I heard a motor bike circling round behind me and into view came Soupy, on that marvellous Honda.

"Lift, Gatesy?" she called out.

Boy, was I glad to see her. I leapt on to the back. Only – well, like this film where the cowboy hero, stuck in a tight spot, whistles up his horse and drops through the window on to his back, but this horse is a joker and at the last minute he moves . . . well, it was similar. Soupy decided to inch a bit nearer just as I sprang out of Anna's grasp . . . and I missed, oh hell – it hurt. However, Soupy managed to haul me up, winded and dying, without laughing too much. On to the bike and away we roared, me holding on tight to Soupy with one hand, and also waving Anna goodbye. She seemed to be having some kind of fit on the pavement.

Soupy had to drop me round the bend, because I hadn't got a helmet.

"I'll carry one for you next time," she grinned.

"Gee t'anks, Soupy. I needed that. Can I buy you a coffee or something?"

"Nah. Got a date with a guy. Steady, straight and faithful. Try it some time. See you, Squeaky." She rode on laughing her head off.

Chapter Five

What a day. Feeling like a dispirited rat I mooched on vaguely, heading for the Club or the Caff, both in the same direction, handy. It was starting to rain which added to the general hilarity. I moved along at a fair rate of knots kicking the odd bit of detritus that happened in my path, until I took on a large pebble which won, knocking the living daylights out of my big left toe. But it pulled me up short. As I hopped in pain I knew I couldn't let these petty incidents get me down. So, I was having trouble with birds; so, what's new? I'd always had trouble with birds. Birds are troublesome that's why, but you just have to put up with that to get what you want. And Mum had pushed off and she was the only person you'd (except for Lynne, of course) possibly bother to save if you saw them drowning in a lake; still, *I'd* survive all right and it would serve the rest of 'em right, bunch of pillocks.

Moi, Patrick Gates, Entrepreneur, Future Millionaire, Whizz Kid, mustn't let life get him down. Be positive, Boyo. Git on your Bike. Visit the Girl.

So I headed towards the upmarket end of town where Lynne lived, where the rich hang out, making my way towards that particular Avenue that's a dirty word in the part of the world where I live, the quiet tree-lined Avenue with the silvery glades and the large gardens, the lawns and the swimming pools,

Lynne Country now, Gatesy Country in the future.

The drive in front of me was bigger than the whole of Constance Place. Just for a minute I hesitated, but not for long, not Moi, even though the house at the end of the drive was much bigger than I'd imagined, as I sauntered whistling past the laurels and the lollipop flowers. I rang the bell which echoed far away. So that's what perfect paintwork looks like, I registered. No answer. I waited. I wasn't bored. The Porsche parked further on was worth contemplating and confirming my view that what you need most in this life is money. Leave the meaning of what's it all about to other people. I'll just take the money. I waited. No one came. I stepped back down the steps and out of the pillared porch.

"Psst," came a voice from up above. I looked up and there staring down at me, pssting and sticking out its tongue, was a face that made Pip Emma's look refined.

"Get lost, worm," it announced and banged down the window. As I stood there shaken, someone answered the door. A woman. And we were in Dynasty land. She wore a dress that draped, a rosy colour, and jewellery that sparkled – it really dazzled – (poor old Chell with your bits and bangles, you don't know the half). She was very thin with a hand-carved and decorated face that just happened to be beautiful. I've seen faces like that in those old movies and thought they didn't make them any more. She just wasn't for real, with more than a touch of the Morticia Adams, and I nearly cut and run right then. I wish I had. But then she spoke and it was all too late. It's almost always too late.

"Hell-o." Her voice was right down there and

seemed to have difficulty making its way out of her throat, a throat that had smoked a thousand cigarettes and forgotten more sins than ever I'd encounter in a million years especially if I stayed at Constance Place.

"Lynne in?" I managed, smiling stupidly.

"Linen? Oh, the laundry boy. Come in, please, and I'll show you where the basket is. It's too heavy for me to carry."

It would be. "Yes, I'll help you," I whispered, and was inside before I remembered that the last thing I wanted was laundry.

The hall was flagged black and white, and pictures hung here and there that bore no resemblance at all to that Chinese girl picture or that poster of the tennis girl scratching her bare bottom. All my outlook changed as I stood there. Only a piece of sculpture rang a bell, eyes and a long neck, something Egyptian it reminded me of. All this and more I gobbled down as if I'd been hungry all my life in Constance Place, and oh, boyo, I had.

"Can you man-age it?" she asked, pointing at a basket just inside a kitchen that was all your dreams – well, not mine – but if your dreams are kitchens, not the space lab. sort but where a fire glowed and bright plates gleamed against wood, it was all there. I couldn't take in any more. I was so mesmerized that I picked up the basket, then plonked it down and said all in a rush:

"I'm not the laundry boy. I've come for your daughter, Lynne. At least I think she's your daughter isn't she?"

"Oh, Lynne." She smiled and her face cracked into humanity. "Of course, you must be one of her friends. No, I'm sorry she's out. Look, come in and talk to me."

I nodded and followed her, hypnotized, my reflection gazing back solemnly at me from an enormous mirror hung in gilt. I smiled at it to make it feel better. Oh cool. You're all right, Gatesy boy. And followed her. I'd been lying all along. It wasn't the house I was looking at, it was her. She moved as if she was on marionette strings operated by somebody up above who didn't like her very much. Her skirt ruffled and ruffled with her movements, and she had these boobs, oh Lord, help me now. Trying to look as if this was all everyday stuff for me I followed her into this incredible room where she motioned me on to a chair. When I sat down my knees ended up higher than my head. I could die there and no one would know.

"Whisky, Martini, gin?"

"Whisky, please."

Life with Uncle Arnold had taught me that what she poured liberally into my glass was only the best. I took a gulp. The windows opened on to lawns that fell away from the house, merging and blurring with the flowers and leafy trees into a green haze. Oh never-never land, the only thing you have in common with Constance Place is that you're both on the same planet, just as Lynne's mother and my old dear were only alike in being both women.

"So you're one of Lynne's friends?"

"I've only just got to know her."

"What do you think of her?"

"I think she's a lovely girl."

The plastic face looked animated for a minute.

"We're new. I want her to get to know people and be happy here." Her voice was wistful. The whisky was causing both her and the room to float a bit. The dragons on the Chinese screen moved their tails as she poured out another quadruple. You could have bought our house with that screen, I guessed. And I also realized that Lynne's mum had the same problem as Uncle Arnold only she was quieter about it.

"Tell me, what do you do?"

"I'm at the college here. And I help out in a paper shop at the week-end."

"What do you do at the college?"

"Business studies."

"Oh, interesting. What do you intend to do with them?"

Her voice might be husky and croaking and she might look like someone out of *Dynasty* but her conversation was just like the old bag next door who's always asking me if I'm ever going to be able to get a proper job when I leave school. But the whisky was making me speak truths.

"I haven't a clue. But I do know I want to make loads of lolly, a lot of money. I'm not getting trodden down under on this loony bin planet."

"Loony bin planet?"

"This one. The Asylum of the Universe. All the nutters in creation are here. That's the only way I can account for it. The only way it makes sense. We're all stark, raving bonkers. I wrote a poem about it once."

"Oh, you write poetry, do you? Lynne used to write poetry. At least she probably still does. Only she doesn't show it to me any more."

"I only wrote that one," I told her, registering that Lynne liked the odd sonnet or so, did she? In which case I'd better get scribbling.

She smiled at me as she poured us out yet more

whisky. The marionette strings were working more smoothly now. Oiled.

"What I really want to do is make lots of dough, money. Go places."

"It's so hard for you young ones nowadays. In my day, well, it was hard, but different. At least if you lost your job one day you could get another the next."

"But surely, you never had to work."

"I did all sorts of things." The smiles were much easier now. "Tell me, do you young ones spend hours arguing about platonic friendship as we used to do?"

Now, Patrick has never gone in for platonic friends in the whole of his life. I mean, what are girls for? If it's conversation I want I go talk to Wally or one of my old mates. Women, well, let's face it, they're just really there for one reason. Until they grow old, of course, like Mum – then they usually run everything anyway. The nearest I get to a platonic friendship is a platonic hateship with Soupy Lethbridge. That's all right because I'd never fancy her in a thousand years.

"No," I came up with, not very inspired.

"No, I suppose not. Not in this permissive era."

"But it isn't a permissive era, not today. We're in the grim eighties not the swinging sixties. That was the time, hippies, beads, rock, sex, psycho – I can't say it . . ."

"You mean psycho-cho . . . I can't say it either." We were both giggling. "All those swirling colours. I had a dress made in them. I must have looked like a walking rainbow. Psychedelia – that's it."

"Yes, that's it."

"But it wasn't really like that. There's far more drugs and sex today. Isn't there?"

Somewhere a warning bell was sounding in my wuzzy head.

"I – I don't really know . . ."

"Do you take drugs?"

"Me? No. I'm not a walking dustbin and that stuff's lethal."

"But I bet you know people who do. Someone like you would."

Every syllable in that husky voice caressed and flattered me. I was great.

"Yeah, yeah. My brother Mike . . ."

The phone rang, jangling jingling . . . She picked it up. And I got up to escape before sweat stuck me to that chair for ever. I moved to the door smiling, head swimming. Put your feet in the right place, boyo.

"Ekky, darling," she was saying, "how wonderful. She put her hand over the mouthpiece and motioned me to stay, but I was half-way down the hall before she caught up with me.

She opened the door smiling. The puppeteer who operated her had really got the hang of it now and she moved like a dancer, her skirt rippling. Outside it was dark, I noticed vaguely. She stood in the doorway and it was all Hollywood corn. I could hardly breathe.

"Might throw a party for Lynne. When we've settled down a bit. If so, I'll get you to help me. What's your name?"

I told her.

"Irish?"

"No. Just Patrick. After an uncle."

"Goodnight, Rusty. Come again."

I ran down the drive. I thought I heard a wolf-whistle from above but I didn't stop to check. The rain had stopped. It had been a hard day. All I wanted was my pit and sleep. I loped along the Avenue. The streets were quiet, no one about, except a couple entwined round one another. Round the corner it dawned on me that it was Wally and Lynne. I lifted up my head and yelled, "Don't forget the legs!" My voice re-echoed through the late evening as I ran.

Dad was walking Zebedee up and down when I got in. He looked grey and ten years older.

"Pip Emma's waiting up for you. To say goodnight she says. But hang on to Zebedee a minute while I get a fresh nappy."

"No, let that cow, his mother, do it."

"Well, don't forget Pip Emma, lad."

"Pip Emma can go throw herself in a lake."

But I put my head round her door.

"Come here," she instructed, sitting up. I approached with care. Arms wrapped themselves round me. I unwound them.

"Don't let this get to be a habit, horrible," I hissed, lest the more revolting figure in the other bed wake up with its bangles and beads.

"Goodnight, Rusty," Pip snuffled, and then, "Shut up, Chell."

I left rapidly, heading for my pit where I most wanted to be, oh, that whisky, oh everything, just too much, I'd sort it out tomorrow, tomorrow, tomorrow.

Chapter Six

I came to, shouting, "Not me, not me," having woken myself up. And whatever that dream was about I didn't want it, no, thank you very much. From where I lay the world held little appeal anyway. That wasn't the duvet I was wearing on my head, it was a hangover. And I remembered the work I was supposed to hand in to old Critchley, and what was it he'd said last time? Something about if I didn't get this lot done, then he'd make it his personal duty to see that I was slung out on my ear, which he would have done ages ago, only no one in the whole benighted establishment ever had enough sense to listen to him. He'd then uttered something about "ignorant, arrogant layabout whose only activity went on below the belt," and removed himself. Yes, I'd better do something about old Critchley.

And I'd got to programme some stuff for the word processor, as well. But in fact the only words I'd be able to process that morning would be unprintable.

But it wasn't that that was quarrying to and fro in my brain like an earwig chewing its way from one side of my head to the other (a terrible fear I'd had when little, caused by Mike, who else? telling me that earwigs ate their way from one ear right through to the other one) no, there was something beyond hangovers, work I hadn't done, trouble with females, oh, no, no, no, I'd remembered the real cause of the gloom. Mum had shoved off . . . and it would be all hell let loose downstairs. I groaned and burrowed down the bed as far as possible and decided not to get up at all. The world shouldn't find me. I'd stay in bed for ever. That'd shake 'em. On second thoughts, no, it wouldn't, they were too used to Mike, who hardly ever got up before four in the afternoon, who was having a love affair with his bed.

At that moment Chell burst in, shrieking and shouting and jangling. She pulled down the duvet under which I was sheltering and I could see she was wearing a baby doll nightie which made her look like the latest in pipe cleaners and as if this wasn't bad enough, she was carrying Zebedee, all beams, dribbles and sopping wet nappy. Chell pulled back the rest of the covers and plonked him down beside me.

"You're not to say those words, Mum says," she shrieked.

"Then, take him away. He's soaking and he stinks."

"Agagagagagagag," drooled Zebedee, banging me with his tiny fists.

"Take him to his mother, for Heaven's sake. He's nothing to do with me."

"She's going with Dad to bring back Mum and they've told me to tell you to get up . . . ouch, don't you hit me . . ."

"I'm not hitting you, you fool, only stop waving that creature in my face at this hour . . ."

"It's not this hour, it's getting late, and Nat says you've got to get us off to school, me and Pip, and look after Zebedee and Gramps . . ."

"Now, birdbrain, get out of here, before I kill you and your unlovely sister. Tell them, her and Dad, to

37

forget about whatever plot they're hatching and wait for me to decide. Got it clear?"

"Yes, Rusty."

"Now get out. And don't call me Rusty. And take Nat's brat with you."

Downstairs was chaos. Two dozen road maps, all of them out of date and useless, lay on the table among the remains of a breakfast. Dad and Nat were in consultation.

I spoke. "Wouldn't it be better if I went with you, Dad? Nat's hopeless, you know she is. Besides, she ought to be going to work, and who's going to look after the kid – you know, the one she never thinks of?"

"Look, bighead, I can drive. I passed my test, remember? And I'm a woman, aren't I? It's not a very good idea for you and Dad to turn up at Greenham. They might not let you past the gate or whatever's there."

I had to admit that she'd got a point, so I made a cup of instantly awful coffee to revive me.

"But I'm not looking after your kid," I spluttered on tasting it. "You'll have to get a baby-minder. Mike."

"I'm not leaving my kid with Mike! I wouldn't leave any kid with Mike."

"You could be right."

I threw away the charcoal that the toaster had contemptuously chucked out, having hung on to it till the last possible moment.

"You do it, Patrick. Honestly, Zebedee likes you much better than me. And you can handle Gramps."

"It just happens that I've got to be at college today. I have a career too, you know."

"One more day off won't matter. Not with your record."

"What about Chell? Let her look after him."

Chell screamed. "It's the school trip today. We're going to the theatre. I've been looking forward to it for absolute WEEKS. And it's paid for."

"Take the kid with you and Dad. That's what Greenham's all about, init? Wimmin with kids and brats living in the mud."

"Look, we don't know where we're going, or what we're doing when we get there except looking for Mum. We might have to walk. We can't take Zebedee."

"Lad, do your bit for me," sighed Dad, uttering at last.

"OKOKOKOKOKOKOKOK. Yeh, but don't think I'm pleased about it. Oh, hell, let's see. I don't have to hand in my work till twelve – in fact I've got to do most of it before I hand it in – then I bet I can get some bird to look after Zeb for you . . ."

"Take care who you pick," snapped Nat.

"Any old scrubber would be an improvement on its mother . . ."

A rapping sounded from above.

"That's Gramps. You get him downstairs, lad, and I'll explain what's happening. I hope he's not upset," blethered Dad.

"Upset," I screamed. "Him upset. What about me? What sort of life is this? Baby-sitting and stopping old fools from getting upset? Plus that uncle of mine, Arnold. I suppose he's up there."

"I heard him come in last night. I think he's all right, though he did fall down the stairs."

"Don't tell me. I don't want to know."

Rap, rap, rap again.

"I'm coming," I yelled. "All right, I'll be mother for

the day. Push off all of you. But just get Mum back. Before I go crazy."

"Before we all do," put in Dad.

"I don't care about the rest of you. It's *Moi* I worry about. All right. Go. What are you waiting for? Patrick's here. He will cope. He will feed Gramps, dear lovable Gramps, he will wake up lovely Arnold in time to get him to work, he will get up Mike to draw his dole money. Chell will go to school, suitably dressed with all her clothes on, and Pip with all her precious homework ready . . . where is Pip? I thought it was quiet . . . Pip! Pip!"

Rap rap rap sounded again, but I took no notice as I searched for Pip. It was just possible that she'd decided to set off for Greenham on an early train.

But no, in the end we found her. On the back seat of the car, wearing wellies, loads of clothes and a determined expression, she would not be moved. She had a packed lunch and a blanket with her. And in the end she went with Dad and Nat. It was easier than dragging her out of the car, as she'd tied a rope round her legs and the front seat. "Let her have the map," I said. "She's the only one who can read."

"Just you remember to ring the school to tell them she's ill or something, brother dear," snapped Nat, winding up her window.

I turned back to the house. Where Chell was having a screaming fit for someone had pinched all her pocket money. "Pip," she yelled, "that Pip."

"Shut up," I said, "and creep into Uncle Arnold's room and get his wallet from the side of the bed. He always leaves it there. I'll put it back later."

"Suppose he wakes up?" whispered Chell, her eyes like saucers, very ugly saucers.

"He never does. Not before eleven."

At last she left. I washed and fed Gramps. I bathed and fed Zebedee. I let in Loopy to stir Mike in time to sign on, he was due for an interview, she said. So he washed for a change, cheers. I hoovered, made the beds, emptying Uncle Arnold out of his after replacing the wallet. Then I took three tins of meat and two tins of veg and stirred them together in a huge stew. I thought it might be low on vitamins and flavour so I poured in tomato sauce, chutney, soy sauce, sweet and sour, and Worcester. It tasted vile. "Good," I crooned to it.

Next I saddled up Zebedee in his buggy. He liked that. Gurgles. However, he looked terrible as dressing babies is not one of my strong points. But of course, I'd also got to take Gramps to the Old People's Centre so I told Loopy to stay with Zebs till I got back. I raced Gramps down the road as fast as I could run, impeded as I was, and he was very angry, but at least it stopped him going on about bringing back hanging for Greenham women. Conscription's the answer he bawled as I pushed him through the door and left him to his cronies.

Back at the house, Loopy, all woman for a change, had changed Zebedee's get-up and he certainly looked better, almost normal, in fact.

"Hey, that's good. Loopy, I wish you'd have him for me. That'd be great. And it'd be something you can do, Loopy."

I couldn't get over Loopy being able to do something. Neither could she. She turned almost pale pink instead of off-yellow.

"I'd love to. I love babies. But I gotter get Mike to Harpenden House for his interview. They're awfully shitty if they want to see you and you don't turn up.

And he's in bad shape today. You know what he's like. I can't manage him and the baby. But I'll come back here, later on when it's finished, Rusty."

She was smiling at me, making me distinctly nervous. I didn't fancy Loopy fancying me, if you know what I mean. Not with Mike around. The trouble is he treats her so meanly that she's just ripe for anyone who's even moderately polite.

"Great. Here, take him while I get some work done."

I settled down but she followed me, holding Zebedee, all you need as you try to cram three weeks' work into an hour.

"Soupy says you could be bright if you made more effort."

"Does she? Huh."

"Soupy's clever. We're not a bit alike." She lapsed into silence, but not for long. "Rusty?"

"What?"

"Soupy says . . ."

"Look, I don't give a twopenny ha'penny damn what Soupy thinks, says or does, just shut up, willya?"

"Rusty, you've made Zebedee cry."

"Belt up!"

"I don't think you're very kind, Patrick. You should be more like Michael. Michael's kind to me . . ."

I picked up my stuff and pushed off upstairs.

Later I set off for college, pushing the buggy. Before I left I checked the date to make sure I'd got old Critchley's deadline right. By chance I read the day's saying.

"Our modes of living are not agreeable to our imagination." (Flaubert.)

That guy knew what it was all about, I muttered as I heaved the buggy down the steps.

Chapter Seven

They came in droves. I knew they would. Gooing and cooing and drooling, isn't he gorgeous, wow, wheredidya get him, you poppet. I headed for the coffee bar with the entourage.

That was the female half of the crowd. The male – well, what *they* said I won't repeat, when did you get caught, lover boy, being the general idea. I found someone to hand in my work to old Critchley (quite a nice chick that one, I can never remember her name and she isn't much to look at, but I'll give her a whirl one day – when I can find the time) and settled back to hear the latest scandal, while the girls played worshipping games with Zebedee.

After a bit the little chick came back with a message from old Critchley saying that I either visit him pronto, that is if I could spare a moment of my valuable time, or he would arrange an appointment for me with the Principal. So I had to go, leaving Zebedee with the girls, because I couldn't really face what old Critchley would have to say if I took him with me. The next half hour or so was not pleasant, so I won't dwell on it, old Critchley's got a vicious tongue and I came away having made all sorts of promises that surprised me, and that I didn't have a hope of keeping. From the self-satisfied smirk on his antique mug, I'd guessed that was his intention, then he really could get me slung out.

I made my way back whistling to the coffee bar crowd, and Lynne was there with them. Unfortunately so was Wally with his arms wrapped round her, revolting, him beaming all over his podgy fat mug (talk about a weight problem) as if he'd just laid an egg.

I just happened to look at my face in the corridor mirror on the way and I couldn't help but feel that Lynne must see a difference between Wally and me. So I took my place at the centre of the crowd – someone scurried away to get a coffee – and turned on the wide, all the choppers gleaming, smile. She did a bit of a cherry, always a good sign. Wally looked nervous, as well he might.

"Not run into you lately, Wally boy. Busy?"

"Yeah," he muttered, gazing at Lynne, who was looking very tasty like one of those concoctions super chefs knock up on the telly.

"I'll look you up some time."

"Well, Patrick, I'm fairly well tied up just now."

"I can see that. Lucky guy. By the way, how are the legs?"

"The legs? What the hell are you talking about?"

Lynne had gone pinker and was sitting up a bit instead of lounging against him.

"Sorry, Wally, if I've said something I shouldn't have," I apologized. The crowd's ears were all bent in our direction. Wally was glaring in a bewildered fashion.

"OK, I won't mention it again. Nor the full moon. A girl like Lynne wouldn't take any notice of little things like that . . . Would you, Lynne?"

"I don't know what you're talking about."

"Right, right, if that's how you want it . . ."

44

Wally unwrapped himself and came near to me.

"Gatesy, what are you up to, you rotten . . .?"

"Nothing, dear lad, why should I be? We're mates, aren't we?"

"I just know, Gatesy, that no good ever came of knowing you. That's what I've found out."

"Want to make something of it? Seems a pity when I've always been on your side, never let you down . . ."

I stood up. Wally's a little guy.

"Got to go now, folks. See you."

I extracted Zebedee from his worshippers and strapped him in his buggy. Then I gave Lynne a special smile, the one Tracey Brewer taught me years ago, and I've practised in the bathroom mirror since. Lynne came up with a cherry that was the prize fruit of the season.

Homeward bound I whistled my head off. It wouldn't be long now. But something else was long. Back at home, there was nobody in. The house felt like the last on a deserted planet. I didn't want to fetch Gramps till I had to. Chell had said she would be late, Arnold was working, and who cared where Mike was, except that Loopy had said she'd take over Zebedee for a bit. I mooched through the house, restless, ill at ease. I stirred the stew and tasted it, revolting. I'd get myself some chips instead as I'd no intention of eating it. I put on the radio.

I wanted to know how they'd got on at Greenham. In the meantime, I'd change Zebedee, and settle him with some toys. And the door bell rang. I rushed to open it. And wished I hadn't. It was old Ma Clements round the corner. She rabbited on and on for hours. Mum was gonna sort out some forms for her, apparently. When I finally got rid of her there were two more at the door asking for Mum. After that there was a steady stream of old bags and young tarts, all looking for Mum, who seemed to be some kind of neighbourhood witch-doctor.

I told them all she'd be back soon, and for some unknown reason this started Zebedee off and he yelled the place down. I walked him up and down, tried to give him some bottle, but nothing would pacify him. I investigated to see if he'd got a pin sticking in him, but no. I sat down with him, knackered out suddenly, and he fell asleep there and then, tear-stained, with podgy mitts clutching me. I sat there for ages as every time I moved he stirred and cried. In the end I was able to sneak him to his cot. And found I was starving, with absolutely nothing I fancied in the house. I had to get to the takeaway. But I couldn't leave Zebedee. This was crazy. I was a prisoner. Suppose it's all right for mothers and so on, but this was awful. I'd go barmy, stuck day after day because of a baby. For the first time ever I had a bit of sympathy for Nat.

I was just deciding to risk it and make a speedy dash to the takeaway, when the door opened and Mike came in, wild-eyed and nutty, followed closely by the bony figure of Loopy. At first Mike didn't make sense, until I told him to take it slowly and tell me what had gone on. He just snarled, threw his hands in the air and rushed upstairs.

I turned to Loopy. Even she has more sense than Mike.

"Did they tell him at the interview that he'd got to get a job and the shock proved too much?" I asked, making cups of coffee.

"Don't be horrible. I can't stand it."

"What's up, then?"

"The police picked him up, didn't they?"

"I don't know." Loopy turning everything into a question always drives me round the bend. "I wasn't there, was I?"

"They said he'd got stuff on him. You know . . ."

"Yes, I know. And had he?"

"No, but they kept him there for ages. He's upset."

"Yeah, I can see that. But he's OK. They let him go."

"Yes. But he thinks someone's ratted on him. And he'll get more aggro. Again. Who would rat on Mike, Rusty?"

"Oh, I dunno. I don't know all his awful friends."

"He doesn't see them much these days. I don't think it's them."

"Anyway, Loop, stay here with Zeb while I fetch some food, will you?"

"Mm. Where is he? Upstairs. But, Rusty, Mike won't get in serious trouble, will he? He's so scared."

"So are we all," I answered, heading for the door, the world outside and food.

"Not you, Rusty. You're not scared of anything."

"I tell you what scares me. The thought of starving to death. I'm off."

I didn't go out that evening. After I'd fetched Gramps, who carried on alarmingly about the stew, I didn't feel like going anywhere. It was late when Dad, Nat and Pip arrived home. They hadn't caught up with Mum. They hadn't been able to find her. Even Pip was subdued.

"Well, what's it like?" I asked.

"I can't even begin to tell you," said Dad, tucking

into the stew. Nat was phoning up her new bloke.

"I can, Rusty. I shall tell you everything," said Pip, but then fell asleep, her head on the table, just like that.

Chapter Eight

I was waiting at the test centre for my examiner to arrive. There were two other pairs of instructors and pupils, and both of the pupils were exchanging nervous remarks, at which I inwardly sneered. Pathetic, I thought. I didn't need anyone else to boost my confidence, thank you very much.

I'd just had my warm-up lesson beforehand in which I drove with the usual skill and ease. My instructor had said to me, "I have every confidence that you will pass first time." I had a feeling that this was his set speech, but who cares, I didn't need his reassurance. I knew I could pass. Dead easy.

The examiner arrived. He had the voice of a robot.

"Mr Gates, would you please sign here?"

"Are you sure you wouldn't just like to give me my pass certificate now and save both of us any bother?"

He didn't reply, humourless nerd, and my instructor frowned at me and the two other candidates tittered, wallies, both of them.

The last thing my instructor had said to me in the car park of the test centre, our pre-examination chat, was, "Lad, I won't wish you luck because you don't need it, but don't give the examiner any of your usual lip. He might object." I thought that I'd just be my normal self. I wasn't going to get intimidated by the whole thing. Not Patrick Gates, Moi.

"Do you suffer from any disability?" asked the examiner.

49

"Well, apart from my glass eye and my pacemaker, I'm in pretty good shape really."

He said sharply, "Just answer the question properly, please."

"Do I look disabled?"

I could see he hadn't taken to me at all, but then examiners aren't supposed to be biased and I thought it an insult to Moi, being asked if I was disabled.

Next was the eyesight test, which was a piece of cake.

"Are you sure this is far away enough?" I asked, to which he replied:

"Just read the number plate, please, Mr Gates."

So I read it and he answered in his horrible robotic voice:

"Your eyesight is satisfactory, Mr Gates."

As we walked to the car he said:

"You may enter the car, Mr Gates, and make yourself comfortable. Drive off when you are ready, turning left at the gate."

Trust my luck to get this humourless bloke as an examiner, I thought as I got in the car, for the way he said, "Mr Gates" was really getting on my nerves. I was glad I'd only got about half an hour of him, as he was obviously trying to make the whole thing as unpleasant as possible. The test itself should be dead easy. The only thing I had to worry about was the speed limit. I had a tendency to drive fast.

I did the usual cockpit drill; putting on seatbelt, checking handbrake and neutral before I started the engine. They wouldn't catch me out with that one.

I moved off smoothly as usual, so smoothly that it wouldn't have disturbed a sleeping Zebedee. I used my mirrors and signalled in good time, did the whole boring old M-S-M routine (Mirror, Signal,

Manoeuvre) before turning left at the gate.

The examiner then said, "Mr Gates, please follow the road ahead."

Where else does he expect me to drive, I thought? Does he think I'd reverse backwards down the road?

After some warm-up driving which was dead easy the robot said:

"Mr Gates, will you please pull up to the kerb?"

I did so, using the correct signal, and he continued:

"Now when I give the signal by banging my book, I want you to stop the car as you would in an emergency such as a child running across the road in front of you."

This would be no problem, though I longed to smash my foot on the brake very hard to give him a nasty jolt. But there wasn't any point as the test would only last about another twenty minutes and I didn't want to give him any excuse to fail me, for we had taken a strong dislike to each other.

By observing him out of the corner of my eye, I saw when he gave the signal and completed the exercise with total competence.

"Carry on please, Mr Gates," said the robot-man. I was certain he wanted me to make a cock-up somewhere but I was equally certain he was going to be disappointed.

After some more driving, in which I stopped at a zebra crossing, overtook a cyclist, obeyed the road signs, turned left and right, positioned the car correctly in the road, used the controls expertly, signalled, used my mirrors, stopped and moved away, stopped correctly at the kerb and read other drivers' intentions faultlessly (in my opinion), we came to the second of the exercises.

He told me in his usual voice to stop just before a junction, then to drive just past it. Oh, reversing time, I thought, no problem, and completed the manoeuvre perfectly, stopping for a car going past and finishing up exactly parallel to the kerb, what else?

"Drive on, please, Mr Gates," said the examiner. Did his voice carry just a hint of disappointment?

After some more routine driving, through roundabouts, one-way streets, narrow roads, hill starts, traffic lights etc, we came to the three point turn.

Now this is my speciality. Of course they don't call it a three point turn, they just say turn the car round, but me, I could turn it round on a sixpence if I wanted, so this, of course, gave me no problem. I did it beautifully, at no time touching either kerb.

Then we headed back to the test centre, into the test car park with the sharp right hand turn they give you at the end, nasty for most people, not for me.

As we parked he said:

"Mr Gates, will you please answer these questions on the Highway Code?"

Why doesn't he just give me the pass certificate now, I thought? He doesn't seriously expect me to fail on the Highway Code, does he?

He showed me some traffic signs, which were easy and asked me questions about what causes skidding, where should you not park (horrible that, because of the amount of places where you can't). I answered it all right, though I might have known he'd ask me that one, and the one about what do you do if you miss your exit at the motorway, which was dead easy. I was tempted to say something like I'd reverse and drive back to it, but didn't.

"Finished?" I asked then. "Can I have my pass certificate?" I put out my hand.

He gave me a piece of paper and walked quickly out of the car and away.

Casually I looked at it, all to myself. It was headed "Statement of Failure". At the box headed "Make effective use of mirrors, take effective rear observation well before: signalling, changing direction, slowing down or stopping" was a cross.

I didn't believe it. It had to be a cock-up. I'm always looking in mirrors. I couldn't have failed for that, or anything else. He'd done it out of malice. I'd like to kick that bastard's head in. It's a good job he cleared off quickly. I'd just wasted a fortune on this test. I was gutted.

My instructor walked over to the car, where I sat in a state of shock.

"How did you get on?" he asked. I couldn't reply. He looked at the paper.

"Mirrors," he said. "Didn't you use your mirrors properly?"

I came out of my trance. "What d'you mean?" I yelled. "I always use my mirrors. When have you noticed me not using them in our lessons? I always use mirrors. I've been cheated. I want my money back."

"Come on, lad," said the instructor. "You were over-confident and you made a mistake. When you're calmer you'll admit it."

I couldn't bear to say any more. He wasn't worth talking to. I vowed that I'd join a new driving school.

He drove me home and I got out. He wanted to know if I'd book any more lessons. I didn't reply.

I looked at the front door. I didn't want to go in.

Didn't want to face any enquiries, especially Nat's. I didn't want to join the no-hopers.

I walked off down the road.

I didn't know where to go, what to do, where to hide myself. I couldn't face going in to college. I'd thought I'd be there with all the crowd telling me I was great. I'd even pictured asking Lynne if she'd like a spin . . . yuck, I felt gutted at the memory of the stupid daydreams I'd spun, all wrecked because a robot-examiner had no sense of humour. Because I knew I'd used my mirrors. I always do. I'm a mirror man. He'd just made an excuse so that he could fail me because he didn't like my face, Moi, Patrick Gates.

Trouble was, old Critchley'd said I had to check into college each day or the axe would fall chop-chop, all gone Patrick Gates. And I'd have to meet the crowd some time and break the glad tidings to them, give them a giggle. Patrick Gates failed his test. Didya hear, Gatesy failed? I could just visualize the whole scenario. The nice ones, the little chick whose name I never can remember, would say, "Oh, but everyone always fails the first time, Patrick." But some of the others – oh hell, I'd skip it, why should I put up with a load of aggro? For two pins I'd walk out of college anyway.

But then I turned round and headed for the place. After all, however bad it was, it had to end some time. Besides, I might run into Lynne without Wally for once, chat her up a bit, do the sad spaniel bit, and it could just work, you never know.

Much later I came out of college, all the sackcloth and

ashes finished with. I headed for home, as this obviously wasn't my day and I might just as well include *all* the nasties in it. Tomorrow could just possibly be better. Tomorrow Lynne might be *my* bird, tomorrow some millionaire or other might offer me thousands for my valuable services, tomorrow we might win the pools, tomorrow I'd pass the test . . . tomorrow Mum would come home and things get back to normal . . . grotty but normal.

Meeting my mates had been rotten but with a don't-care-force-field-have-a-giggle-on-me wrapped tight round me I'd survived even though in addition to everything else all my teachers had decided that this was the day to point out the error of Patrick Gates's ways and set him on the right path. I'd let it all go in one ear and out the other but every one of them had given me a fresh pile of work, cheers.

There had been no sign of Lynne, anywhere.

Back at Maison Gates Dad was sitting in a heap crying and repeating:

"Bessie, how could you, how could you?"

When he saw me he broke off to say:

"They're all talking about her. Everybody. My Bessie. They keep saying how sorry they are for me. Rita Bates has made some rock cakes for us."

"Good. Keep them for the next riot. They'll do for missiles."

"Patrick, lad, I'm not sure I can carry on."

"Dad. Dad. Listen. I failed my test."

"Patrick, lad, I'm telling you I can't manage without Bessie. I might do sommat to meself, Patrick lad."

"Well, don't make a mess, will you?"

"Did I hear you say you'd failed?" cried Nat, who was making up her face in a mirror while Zebedee wailed and she took no notice, as usual.

"Yes. Want to make something of it?"

"No. I couldn't care less, I thought you would. You're no good."

"Thank you. Why don't you deal with that child? It probably needs feeding or changing."

"Chell, I'll give you that nail varnish you wanted if you'll feed the brat," cried Nat.

Chell floated in with enough scarves to take off and picked up Zebedee.

"You revolt me, Nat," I said.

"In a queue for shits, you'd be first," she said, shrugging.

"D'ye say you failed your test?" slurred Uncle Arnold. "Have a whisky. But not mine."

"Isn't anyone going to clean up or get a meal ready?" I shouted.

"I've done some chips," Pip called out and went on, "Sorry, Rusty. I think you're a super driver, but like me at school, you were probably too good and people take it out on you. But how are we going to get to Greenham now? Dad and Nat are useless. I want to go with you. What do we do now?"

"Blowed if I know." I felt as if I was going mad. "Anyway, I'm going out. This place gets on my nerves."

"Don't go, Rusty. I promised I'd tell you about the fences and the webs . . ."

"Later, Pip, later . . ." I headed for outside as Dad started to cry again and Zebedee wailed in protest.

I don't know where I went. All places were alike to

me in the black gloom I was in. How could I make my escape from the hell-hole? How could I get away? I'd thought having a driving licence would help. Now it would be ages before I could afford to take the test again.

Get away, get away. I walked into the centre of town, through the emptying streets and out again. Out into the countryside, walking, walking up into the hills and back down again. Somewhere I bought a coffee and sat for ages drinking it. At some pub I drank a lager and then another at another pub.

Lynne, I wanted to see Lynne. I wanted to hold that soft body in my arms. I wanted to cover that gentle face with kisses.

I walked on along the pavement, heading in the direction of her home. Maybe she'd be there, perhaps she'd talk to me. I needed comfort. Even Moi, Patrick Gates, needs comfort at times.

The evening darkened. Twilight lingers long at this time of the year.

The car that drew up beside me was powerful and silent, making me jump. Trouble? That's all I needed. And it was. But not that sort.

The car was a Porsche. A door opened.

"Get in, Patrick. I'll give you a lift."

The voice was husky, the voice of a thousand sins, I thought crazily.

"Oh, yes please, I need a lift," I answered, stumbling in. "Thanks a lot, Mrs Martin."

"Call me Laura," she said.

"Oh yes. I will. Laura," I answered.

And it was all the same, the room, the chair, the whisky.

The whisky made me talk. I told her about failing the test, about college, about how much I wanted to escape from home, how I wanted to make a million and live the good life, how her daughter was going out with a wally and ought to be going out with me . . . told her about Mum going to Greenham . . .

She listened, watching me, not saying much. A few brain cells, not all dead, wondered where was ole man Martin, when did they eat, and what about the kid I'd seen last time who'd psst at me. But I didn't care. I didn't care much about anything. At last she stood up.

"You'd better go now," she said. "It's getting late."

She pulled me out of the chair depths, put her hands round my face and kissed me. It went on and on for a long time. The incredible boobs stuck into me and she smelt – very expensive. At last she let me go and I tottered to the door. She watched me, smiling.

I somehow reached the hall and negotiated the steps and, of course, looked up.

A death's head was watching me. I shot upwards as the mask was pulled off.

"Cretin," the face that had been underneath it whispered and the window slid down.

Why does she let Lynne stay out so late? I wondered, but then who cared in that house? Besides I didn't much want to think about Lynne just then. Tomorrow – tomorrow would be a better day.

Letting myself in quietly I could hear Dad and Gramps arguing. One of them was throwing a wobbly but I didn't wait to find out which one.

Chapter Nine

In the morning Mike is a beastly sight. Everyone else seemed to have gone, leaving the house empty except for us, the breakfast remains and a postcard of the Tower of London – a very old postcard.

"Love to you all. Pip and Chell, be good. Don't worry about me. Might come home next week-end. Mum."

"Oh, that's good," I muttered, wanting my head to clear, and then not wanting my head to clear as memories crowded in that weren't good at all.

"What gets you up at this time of day, Mike? Are you the new family worker?"

Mike snarled, "I'm going for another interview. Y'know I was stopped and searched the other day. So I never got to *that* interview and the stupid DHSS thought I deliberately didn't turn up and they've sent a letter cancelling my dole money. So I've got to turn up and explain."

"That's tough," I said, glad to know I wasn't alone with rotten luck. "Still, you were clean. You didn't have any stuff on you."

"I take care to keep it well hidden," he smirked. I wonder where, I thought, probably in my room, knowing him.

"Isn't Loopy going with you?" I asked. Where was the slave?

"She's gone out with Sister Soupy today," he

growled. "As if that was more important than this."

"I'll come along for a laugh, then. See how the scavengers live."

"Suit yourself," he said. "You won't be so superior when you start claiming."

"That day won't happen for me. I'm gonna be a millionaire."

"Delusions of grandeur. The only way you'll get any dough is by marrying a rich bit. And that's not likely."

As we made our way to the dole office he said:

"I meant to ask you. Where's Mum got to? Haven't seen her lately. D'you know?"

I gaped at him. Was he so far gone he didn't even know she'd gone to Greenham? Never, never would I go on drugs if that's what they did to the mind. I didn't answer. I couldn't bear to do all the explaining.

I looked at him. Was he doped up? I had thought he was slightly more aware before he'd said that. But his mind was back on his old topic.

"If I find out who grassed on me, I'll do 'em," he threatened.

A strange idea flipped in my brain – but I pushed it away – no, not likely, she wouldn't – no, of course not. But had she? I'd said something to Laura about Mike. But why should she? Just for fun?

Eventually we arrived at the dole offices.

"Is this where you get paid for your little stroll down here, then?" I inquired.

"No, pillock," he grunted. "This is the interview place, not the signing on place. You'll get to know them well before long, sunbeam."

I knew the grey unattractive exterior of the building,

but I had never been inside. As we walked in, I saw that the building was basically two large rooms, one with all the chairs in rows, a ticket machine and an interview desk at the end filled with miserable-looking people, and the other, which Mike entered, with chairs spread out and booths numbered 1–10 along a corridor leading off it. It was like a morgue in there.

Mike and I walked to two of the chairs which were empty and near to each other and sat down. The chairs were bolted to the floor and cigarette ends littered the burnt carpet. Gloom lay on it like a grey Army surplus blanket.

"How do you know when it's your turn?" I asked.

"They call out your name and booth number on the loudspeaker," he replied.

I noticed that his suspect memory didn't fail him where money was concerned, only unimportant matters such as Mum leaving didn't click.

Surveying the scenario around the drab surroundings, looking like a daisy in a concrete backyard, I spotted a small blonde who appeared to be on her own, so while Mike was being grilled I thought that I'd while away the time by chatting her up.

Mike, though today he had said more to me than in the past year, had now clammed up and was staring gloomily at the floor, waiting for his name to be called.

At last the loudspeaker broadcast his name. "Mr Gates, Booth No 5." Mike stirred himself and slouched across the room.

"Don't forget to tell them about the building work you've been doing," I shouted to him, loud enough for all to hear.

He turned round and glared at me furiously and made a rude sign before disappearing.

After he'd gone I looked again at the girl. She was still alone so I decided to go over and speak.

"What's a nice girl like you doing in a place like this?" – the old corny chat-up line, probably quite appropriate here.

She smiled nervously at me but didn't reply. Cat got her tongue? Why are the girls I fancy hard to chat up and the girls I don't fancy easy?

"What's your name. Can I buy you a coffee or something?" was my next attempt to break the ice. I thought I'd seen a drinks machine somewhere in this dump.

"Look, you'd better leave me alone." She spoke at last. "My boy-friend's here."

Did she think I was naïve enough to believe that? I'd been here about twenty minutes and nobody had been near her yet. She was just playing hard to get.

"I suppose he's seven feet tall and an all-in wrestler," I suggested.

"No, but he's six feet two and a boxer," she replied.

"Look, shall we cut the crap? Let me introduce myself. I'm Patrick Gates, entrepreneur, future millionaire, nineteen years old . . ." (which was a lie).

A hand tapped my shoulder. Using my sixth sense and observing the expression on the girl's face, I guessed that she hadn't been spinning.

Instead of just turning round and receiving what would undoubtedly have been the blow of the year, I turned and ducked so that the boy-friend's punch collided with a bloke standing behind me, looking bored.

This, however, grabbed his attention. He stopped looking bored. With a yell he repaid the compliment to the boy-friend, who was indeed six feet two, but his adversary was even bigger, which took the boy-friend's attention off me, as he had enough to cope with at that moment. They both had.

This was, however, only part of the scenario. For as those two exchanged blows, all their friends decided to join in to make it a Western-style punch up.

So that's why the chairs are bolted down, I thought. At least that lot couldn't use them, so it was pretty much a case of unarmed combat. I edged myself well out of the fighting zone and stood in the doorway watching with the other pacifists, some of whom, along with the dole officials, were probably phoning the police.

I was just on the point of leaving, lest someone pointed me out as the instigator of this fracas, when Mike emerged from the corridor leading to the room, with a black look on his face. The moment he entered he was punched in the head by one of the combatants, and if he had been in a bad mood before, he was in a filthy one now. After recovering from the shock, he aimed a well-placed kick at his opponent. Mike can fight a bit when roused.

I took off. If Mike was stupid enough to get mixed up in this, I wasn't going to help. Besides, the police would be here any minute. The mêlée was quieting down a bit now, with a couple of bodies lying comatose on the floor. I left just in time to see Mike splatted by some giant.

I think the world's gone mad sometimes, what with all this just for talking to a girl and Lynne preferring Wally to me. Everything's bananas.

63

I did wonder if Mike would get caught. Stupid idiot. With his record he could get put away. Oh well, that was his worry. And if he got put away it might cure him of his drug problem. In the unlikely event of his naming me, I'd never been there. Why would I be going down the Social, if I wasn't claiming?

Chapter Ten

That night the ceiling fell in on me.

I'd just gone off to sleep, and was participating in a multi-love-in with girls stroking me and murmuring how wonderful, superb, fantastic, incredible, dynamic, sexy, handsome, witty and clever this guy Patrick Gates was when c-c-c-rump! I awoke to find half a ton of lath, plaster and choking dust covering me like a bed-cover.

This is it! Four minutes, they said. Is that dust radioactive? I'm too young to die.

I leapt out of bed – well, crawled out from under the grot heaped on it. This gave me time to realize that the Nuclear Winter wasn't about to begin, it was Constance's ceiling falling in.

What was I going to do? I looked at my watch – half past two. No one, least of all me, was going to mend a ceiling at 2.30 in the morning. A few more bits of dingy plaster and moulding dropped off in a half-hearted kind of way and that was that. I seized the duvet and lobbed the debris on the floor. Then I fell back in and went to sleep. But the lovely girls had gone. Ole Critchley had taken their place, slagging me off for all the work I hadn't done which would fill container lorry after container lorry according to him. He set me on catching up. I woke up knackered.

The disasters that have always circled the airspace above Constance Place, leering, sneering, looming

65

and glooming, decided to have a whirlwind that week. Maybe it was only Mum who'd held them at bay, anyway.

Dad set off for Greenham again – on his own this time – ran into a cloudburst, the car broke down, and tinkering with it in the downpour he got soaked to the skin, returning to home and bed chilled, soaked, shivering, moaning, "Bessie".

Uncle Arnold volunteered to mend my ceiling and succeeded in bringing the lot down. I moved my bed on to the landing and slept there instead. While we were trying to find someone who would do the job for as little as possible Mike left the bath taps running – he was taking his annual – water overflowed down the stairs and poured through the living room ceiling as well.

"We're jinxed," Mike growled.

"I'm sick of ringing up people," Nat complained. "And I'm sick of nursing Dad. Why doesn't somebody else do something as well as me?"

"Tell Loopy to do it."

"You tell her."

"I've got problems," snarled Mike.

He had, too. He hadn't yet been picked up by the police, but it was only a question of time, Sergeant Andy Baker had informed him. They were at school together, when Mike was the bright boy and Andy the thickie. As Andy rose steadily in the Police Force, Mike sank lower and lower.

"You shouldn't be such an idiot," Nat said. "You create your own problems."

"Belt up."

"See here, worm. I'm not Loopy. You don't speak to me like that."

It was Chell who cried out. She was nursing Nat's baby and watching soap, as usual.

"Why is Zebedee covered in spots?"

He'd been grizzling for some days, but then he'd never really stopped since Mum left. No one had taken much notice.

Now we moved over to investigate.

Chell was right. Zeb had more spots than skin.

Next day, so had Chell.

"Why don't we just paint the door with a red cross and Lord Have Mercy on us?" Nat moaned. She'd had to have time off from her job, and this made her furious, through mad passion not for work but for her managing director with whom she was having an affair. She'd have moved to higher spheres ages ago except for the free baby-minders at 17 Constance Place. I'd seen her bloke, a nasty all-executive type with a Jag, a blonde fortyish wife and kids at boarding school. I did say to her once that if she thought she'd get anywhere with him she'd lost her marbles. He'd never divorce that hard-faced bitch of his, who incidentally lived about four doors away from the Martins in Sylvan Avenue.

"I wouldn't marry *him*," she snapped. "I'm not marrying any *man*." (Rhinoceros, cheetah, matron? Perhaps she'd trot up the aisle with a hippo?) "All I want is a comfortable flat and a full-time nanny for Zebedee."

"What, in this town? Everybody'd know about it. Besides, I'm not sure you're worth that much on the market."

She smirked.

"Little do you know, brother. You didn't get *all* the fatal charm."

In the meantime we entered Loopy in the nursing stakes. She looked after Dad quite well. After a few days' weep in bed, he got up, put on his dressing gown, came downstairs and taught her to play crib, while Mike went back to bed, lying there for hours. She also looked after Chell and Zebedee (and of course, Mike).

"There's a lot of work here," she said one day, serving up some burnt chops, for she was a hopeless cook, not being interested in food or ever seeing the need for it.

Next day the washing machine broke down.

And the telly went on the blink

We had to stop Mike from kicking it in. It was Loopy who phoned for another from Rediffusion.

That evening Soupy appeared, a black crow with ear-rings. She took off her leathers and parked herself. Loopy scuttled off to make coffee. We'd all got used to it, but she was still sporting the technicoloured eye Mike had generously given her after the punch-up at Harrington House. He always did this. If he had to suffer, so did she. Soupy frowned, black as thunder, black as her leathers, when she saw it.

Chell and Zebedee sweated spottily on the sofa watching telly, Dad mourned in the corner, Uncle Arn scrabbled in the sideboard, Mike lay on the floor and Gramps held out his teeth. It was decontamination time but his Minder was missing. Mum had escaped.

I could see Soupy warming up to utter, but Loopy lurched into the room holding four mugs of coffee in one hand, most of it dribbling on to the floor. Soupy rescued what was left – then turned down the volume.

"I've seen her," she said.

Mike lifted his unlovely lamps.

"Silly cow walked into my fist. Wanter make somethin' of it?"

"He didn't hurt me, Soups," trembled Loopy.

"I don't mean my sister," Soupy replied coldly. Then added as if she couldn't help it, "You thug."

"Loopy likes it. Don't you, chicken?"

All Loopy's bones jangled as she nodded.

"I do. I do. Mike's really nice to me. He's just got his little ways, Soups."

"None of 'er blurry business," growled Mike.

"Heaven help you both," said Soupy. "But that's not what I came about." She raised her voice.

"Mr Gates. Mr Gates, I've seen your wife. Had a chat with her."

Dad didn't hear. Gramps did.

"Ungrateful woman," he squelched. Failing to make enough impact he rammed his teeth back in, and shouted, "Running away from her duties."

Zebedee's grizzles crescended to screams.

"I can't stand this," Soupy cried. "Chell, give that baby to me. Poor sore thing."

She lifted Zebedee and popped him into a chair.

"He's soaking, poor lamb. Oh lord, so's the chair. What's been happening?"

"Everything's still wet. Mike turned the bath on and forgot he had. He's not used to bathing," I said.

"Watch it, brother . . ." he growled.

"It's come through the ceiling. I'm surprised you didn't notice."

"The washing machine's busted as well. Chell did that. She's incompetent," said Pip, just coming in.

Chell launched herself at Pip, nails for talons.

69

Pip dodged. "You can't claw me. You've bitten them too much, stupid."

"Belt up, you two," I shouted.

"But all that water was lovely. I measured it for my project," Pip shouted.

"Someone in this thieves' den has had me whisky. Again."

Mike turned up the volume as the old stale theme tune from the longest-running soap boomed out.

"Doesn't anyone want to know what I've got to say?" Soupy bellowed. "You lot drive me mad."

"Welcome to the club," I said.

"Soupy, Soupy, tell me about Mum. Is she lonely without me?"

"My poor Bessie. Why did she have to do this to me? She should have told me she was unhappy. She should have told me."

"I'm off. I don't want to hear about that ungrateful bitch. Deserves all she gets," said Arnold, departing.

"Mr Gates – listen – she's all right. She's doing what she wants to do."

But it was like talking to a duvet. You couldn't get through to him.

"She should've told me. Oh my Bessie."

Soupy raised her voice another couple of decibels.

"She sends her love to you all. I spent a day with her. At the Emerald Gate."

"Where?"

Mike woke up with a rush. "The Pearly Gates: Mother Gates at the Pearly Gates." Then in a nearly normal voice he said:

"Where is Mum, by the way? I haven't laid eyes on her lately."

"Soupy, next time you go, take me with you on the

back of your motor bike," Pip said.

"I failed my test," I said, to get the hilarity out of the way.

"So? Everyone does first time," said Soupy, face straight. "You going up to see her then, Mr Gates?"

"To see Bessie? Well, I might, but then what's the point? I didn't know she was unhappy."

I pushed off. If I hadn't I'd have kicked him, then burnt the house down, and you shouldn't go round kicking your Dad or burning houses. Soupy followed.

"Had enough of Home Sweet Home?" I inquired.

"Mine's not much better. Happy family life's a myth, I think."

"Come for a coffee. Sorry I can't give you a lift."

"That's OK. I'll give you one."

"Equality for you."

"There's no equality," Soupy said. "Women are just immeasurably superior to men in both values and attitudes."

I let it go. She's stupid but then they all are and she hadn't sent me up for failing the test.

As we sat drinking coffee she fished a scrap of paper from her pocket.

"Pip gave it to me as we came out. Something she wrote."

"Oh, hell."

"Hey, look."

"Do I have to?"

"I'll read it to you."

"Don't bother."

"My pleasure."

"Oh, get on with it, then."

> "Cats and mothers
> Ribbons and wells
> Snakes and spiders
> Women and benders
> All making their patterns
> Weaving their webs
> Weaving their spells . . ."

"What's all that about? Sounds creepy."

"It's Greenham. Pip's view of it. Funny . . ."

"You lost your marbles, Soupy Lethbridge?" The voice that broke in was anything but poetical and it didn't stop there. "Whizz kid Soupy out with this jerk! Thought you'd got more bloody sense!"

Anna had arrived, Super-glue girl, voice like a loudhailer. How could I ever have fancied her? I got up to go, but she pushed me back on to the seat, her face more like a Red Indian on the war trail than ever. And who was about to be scalped?

Me. Poor me.

No, no. Not poor me. Moi, Patrick Gates, entrepreneur, Whizz kid (not Soupy, *Moi*. How could a mere femme be a Whizz kid?).

I wasn't sure whether Anna intended punching Soupy or me but I didn't intend hanging about to find out. Soupy always could look after herself. So ducking under Anna's arm I headed for the door and ran. Anna's shrieking voice ran after me until I couldn't hear it any more, then I stopped by a lamp-post and got back my breath.

Going back home held all the charm of returning to a high security prison. I knew I'd end up putting Gramps, Zebedee and probably Dad and Chell to bed. And I could think of better things to do with beds than put Gramps, Zeb, Uncle Tom Cobleigh and all into them. The route I took was in the diametrically opposite direction to 17 Constance Place.

She drove the car expertly, rather fast, with all the power, that beautiful power. Power is one of the sexiest things going. "We're getting out of the moronic inferno," she said.

The scenario had changed. Jeans, sweater, trainers, no make-up. She smelt of scented money, monied scent. I sat back as we slid through the town and climbed up the hills, the twisty bends and high backs. She played tapes as we went along. We didn't talk. She didn't seem to want to and I couldn't burble the old jabberwocky to her as I would've to a girl. I didn't know what to say and I wasn't sure I knew what to do, but I was sure I'd do it when the time came for the night was warm and Patrick Gates was on the up and up after a long and draggy day. I trembled a bit but not much.

We sat on the rampart of the old Iron Age fort, Woodbury Hill. Wally and I went there years ago and I pinched his choc bar which we were supposed to keep till we'd eaten our sandwiches and Nat walloped me when he cried. What a weird thing to remember – a rapid replay of an old film in my mind.

The town lay below, lights just starting to come on, but you could still see the spires, the ribbon river, the incinerator, the old gas works, the slummy West

Quarter with Constance Place the jewel in its centre, the railway line, the mini-spaghetti junction of the motorway on the far side.

She lit a cigarette.

"You don't?"

"No."

"No vices?"

"I don't go in for vices."

"Just women, I hear."

"People exaggerate."

"They must have done or from what I've heard you'd be old before your time."

She was laughing at me.

"Still in love with my daughter?"

"Yeah, yeah. But I can't get near her. Wally keeps her shut away."

"Well, you can easily do something about that. He's not competition for you."

"You think I stand a chance?"

"Oh yes."

"I didn't know you had another – daughter."

I hadn't meant to say this. Who wanted to think of the monster in the upstairs room at a time like this?

"Oh, you've met her?"

"She's spoken to me. Funny kid . . . (Round the bend, bonkers, barmy, crazy, nuts, mad, a brick short of a load) . . . a bit of a joker."

"Oh yes, she's that all right. But she's staying with a friend tonight . . ."

"And your husband?" I dared to say.

"Oh, we each live our own lives."

She stubbed out her cigarette and stretched out on the grass. Looking at her I didn't care if she had a bevy of daughters and a stable of husbands.

74

Tracey Brewer, I'm counting on you for help, I thought as I leaned over and moved into over-drive.

Rather later she said:

"You're not still fed up? Frustrated with your life?"

"I haven't a clue what you're talking about."

It was a long, long way from Constance Place who-ever she was.

Chapter Eleven

"We're Absolute Beginners," I warbled into the cracked (bound to be) and spotted bathroom mirror before leaping along the landing which is poky (naturally), and I misjudged its distance, ending up hanging down the stairs, clutching a banister (worm-eaten, of course) which broke.

At the painful bottom of the stairs an apparition loomed over me. It had a red spotted face, spikes of white and cabbage-coloured hair and a spider tattoo over half its forehead.

The pain and the spectacle brought on the dizzies (a weakness I despise) and I had to put my head down to my knees. Far away a muzzy voice whispered:

"D'you like it, Rusty?"

It had to be Chell. I worked hard at looking up and succeeded.

"You look like Caligula starting out on a new batch of murders. Oh, help me up."

Weeping, she helped me up.

"I were fed up wiv being in and spotty," she wailed, spitting and blowing everywhere. "I wanted to look dishy."

"You do. Like bubble and squeak with beetroot."

She wailed louder.

"Belt up, for Gawd's sake. Here, have a dish-cloth."

She wiped her face with the dish-cloth, leaving a trail of tea-leaves all over her nose.

I hobbled towards the kettle, in need of a cuppa.

"What am I gonna do?" she continued to wail. "I look terrible, don't I?"

"Yes."

"Help me, Rusty."

"Look. See Nat. She's not as horrible as she seems. She couldn't be. Get her advice. You can cut the hair. I don't know what to do about the tattoo . . ."

"It's only a transfer."

She wasn't sobbing quite so loudly now.

"That's all right then. Nat'll fix the rest."

She drifted away, leaving me to coffee, Black American funk and peace.

Which never lasts. Not at Maison Gates.

A groan heralded Dad. He still wore his grey elephant-skin dressing-gown. He looked like a depression hanging round the Atlantic, about to move over Iceland, Faroes, Forties, Fisher, Bight and so on.

"I don't think I can tek much more, lad," he moaned.

"You're not the only one . . ."

"What's that, Patrick lad?"

"Nothing, Dad."

"Made the cuppa, 'ave you? Pour some out for me. I need something to pick me up. Nothing like a cuppa in a hard life."

I gave him tea and turned up the music louder. Uncle Arnold joined us, bearing all the world's hangovers on his heavy brow.

"I'll push off," I said, before I got caught for house repairs, ringing Health Centres, plumbers, builders, baby-minding, taking Gramps to the Centre . . .

Besides, I had work to do. I found an empty alcove in

the college library and settled into it. But Laura got between me and old Critchley. I tried to get past her into the world of work but it wasn't on. I just sat and thought about sex. I read this bit in the *Cosmo* magazine warning women that men think about sex six times every hour. It's worse with teenagers. They think about sex ninety-nine point nine per cent of the time, so it's not so surprising they don't do the work they should as that they get any done at all.

I know a lot of women, strange, scrumptious, inscrutable creatures, not quite real – Nat, Soupy, Loopy, Anna – no, let's forget about Anna, and hope she forgets about me – funny little Chell, she was quite sweet this morning looking for help from Big Brother Rusty, but Lynne, I still wanted Lynne, the one that I want, wah, wah, wah. I'd like to sin with Lynne, but Brother Gates, you've been sinning with the wrong person, you didn't sin with Lynne, you sinned with Lynne's Mum. And clear as a bell I heard Mum's voice in the library.

"That wasn't a good idea, Patrick, was it?"

"But, Mum, it wasn't my idea, honest, it wasn't me. It was her."

"The woman tempted me? Adam said that. It's so old it's got whiskers. Like Adam, probably. Boring man. Eve was far more interesting."

"Mum, mum . . ."

But I was in the library and she wasn't. And out of the blue, like a gut pain – I missed her, and I wanted to see her, talk to her. Not just to get her back so she'd sort out bloody awful Maison Gates which didn't make any sort of sense without her but so as she'd be there to have a chat over a cup of a coffee and we'd have a giggle.

Why had she gone? Was it only because she couldn't stand the set-up any longer? What had she used to say about things? I never took much notice at the time. I was usually thinking about the girls – all those girls beginning with Tracey Brewer, Maureen Farrell, Tina Briggs, Ally – Ally somebody, Julia Mason, Fran Parsons, Edie Shore – wow – wow – too hot for me to handle, that one. Then who was next? Mandy, Penny Crew and her identical twin Helen, yeh, yeh, then Anna and now Lynne but why was I so slow moving in on Lynne? I'd never messed about like this before when I'd wanted a girl. Was it loyalty to Wally? No, I didn't have any loyalty to Wally. Wally was too Wally to bother being loyal to. It wasn't that. Maybe I was getting old. Maybe it was Laura really. No, Laura was wonderful but not for me. Too much for me, caviare daily.

Work, do some work, Patrick Gates. You'll never get anywhere mooning about like this. No way to be a millionaire at twenty-one, wasting time on them silly biddy wimmin . . .

Wimmin – Greenham – what's it all about then? Why had Mum gone? She couldn't really suppose her being there would make any difference. What was she looking for. An affair with somebody else besides Dad? Not likely. Not Mum. Not that old – but I suppose having five kids might leave you – reluctant. Besides, you wouldn't go to Greenham for an affair unless you'd gone lesbian. LESBIAN? MUM? No, not the type. Not Mum. But who knows?

Work – must do some work.

Must find out more about Greenham and why Mum went.

Must see Laura *again*.

I love Lynne.

More about Greenham. CND.

The little chick walked into my alcove. You know, the one whose name I can never remember. And her face lit up when she saw me. It always does. She always looks at me like I'm all the goodies that ever happened, which makes me feel like Robert Redford. But she's a very little chick, a bit old-fashioned, looking about twelve, and I'm not into under-age sex. And then – I spotted that she was covered with CND badges, Greenpeace, you name it, she was wearing it. Little Chick was into minority groups.

"Hello, Patrick," she said, beaming at me like I was the first day of Spring and she about to open all her petals. Would she? (No, no, not a good idea.)

"Look," I said, "I see you're a member of CND and various groups."

"Mm. Yes, Patrick."

"Well, I feel I'd like to know more about these things. I haven't taken much interest in the past but since my mother left us all to go to Greenham" (the right sob in the voice) "I feel it's my duty, yes, duty, to find out more about it all. Will you help me?"

"Oh yes, Patrick. I'd help *you* with anything. Just tell me what you want."

"Oh –" (I was gulping a bit, for Little Chick was not quite what she seemed) – "just some literature, pamphlets, you know."

"I know. You'll have everything tomorrow. If . . ."

"If what?"

"If you take me out one evening." And she stretched up, up on her poggy little legs in their woolly stockings, leaned over the table and kissed me on the lips.

Oh Lord, I thought as I naturally responded. She's got a lovely smell and taste – my cup runneth over and is going everywhere and I can't catch it all up.

She'd left the library, glowing. She was going to meet me tonight, bearing all the literature for my perusal. Happy Little Chick. I still couldn't remember her name. It was clear that she was absolutely besotted with Moi. I'd be good to her. But not too good.

Somehow I finished the work, turned up for a couple of sessions and felt hungry, starving, ravenous. I'd eat a decent meal that evening even it if meant cooking it myself. I set off for the supermarket.

And Lynne was there.

All the cans hung upside down and the trolleys danced on a ceiling that shimmered. We both stopped where rainbows hung over the toilet rolls, the air fresheners and the paper towels. She was so beautiful I wanted to lie down there and then to give my all right by the lavatory pongers all hung in lavender and pine.

"Hi, Patrick," she croaked. I'd forgotten how her voice got trapped on its way out of her throat (oh glory, her throat) so that when she spoke it had a husky break in it.

"Lynne."

"I haven't seen you for ages."

"Too long."

"A pity."

"You can always change it."

"How do I do that?"

"You can see me every day for the rest of our lives."

"DO YOU MIND? YOU'RE BLOCKING UP THE GANGWAY."

A crowd of unlovelies had formed around us. Not that we cared. We could have stood there for ever gazing, looking, staring, eating each other up with our eyes while we hoarded each feature against future deprivation.

The crowd muttered and cluttered.

"Let's go," I said and shoved my trolley to the bloke who'd complained, and Lynne's at the woman pushing her crossly from behind.

"All yours, Monsieur, Madame," I bowed, then I seized Lynne's hand and we ran – all the way to the park, to that bench where we'd first sat with the blossom waving all around her.

I'm not going to tell you what we said or did because if you've sat on a bench in the park with the one you love you'll know anyway and if you don't then it's up to you to find out. Enough to say when we came out of the park with Lynne looking like a flower that's had its petals mussed in the wind, she'd promised to finish with Wally and was meeting me that evening.

Back to the shopping. I was still ravenous.

It was only when I reached the corner of Constance Place that I remembered the little chick. It was remarkable that I'd thought of her at all in the state I was in. Better ring her, say I was sorry I couldn't make it and I'd see her in college next day.

But I couldn't ring her. I didn't know her name. I never had. She was the Little Chick, no name. Oh well, some people were just born to be hurt. Couldn't be helped.

Lynne – Lynne.

And I whistled as I let myself into Constance Place.

I soon stopped whistling.

Dad in his elephant skin, Uncle Arnold, looking amazingly sober at this time of day, a business type in a double-breasted, and a policeman all stood in our all-purpose room. I tried to walk out again backwards on tiptoe which isn't easy and which was a waste of time as they all turned round and watched me.

"Patrick, Patrick, come and tell them it's all a mistake," cried Uncle Arnold.

I smiled weakly and said, "I'm sure you don't need me here," but Arnold seized me and hauled me in among them.

"I don't know anything about this . . ."

"No one said you did," said the fuzz, sharp.

Double-breasted business spoke up.

"Mr Gates was found walking out of our store with merchandise he hadn't paid for."

"What?"

"Two bottles of single malt and one of blended."

"Well, it wouldn't be baby food, would it?"

"But I didn't do it," cried Arnold.

"You were carrying them in the inside pockets of your mackintosh."

"Come clean, Arnold. You know what you're like," said Dad heavily, a great help.

"I'm not like anything and I never shoplifted in my life."

The business suit and the fuzz had obviously heard it all before many times. As for me, I only wanted to get away and think about Lynne.

"We shall have to charge you. It's our policy."

83

"Look, I'll pay."

"No. It's too late."

"I'll never use your store again."

"Please yourself."

"Just let me pay."

"No, it's the store's policy to charge offenders."

"I shall call my lawyer. Nothing like this has ever happened to me before."

"You're perfectly entitled to do that."

"And why not phone Aunt Edna while you're about it. She might give you moral support," I cried, full of inspiration, all because Lynne was meeting me, might even be in love with me. No more wallying around.

I flew upstairs on winged footsies, Moi, Patrick Gates was gonna rule the world. Some day. Uncle Arnold's voice followed me.

"You can't charge me! You can't charge me!"

Chapter Twelve

"Chips are fattening
Beans are better,
Lynne's much nicer.
I know, 'cause I ate her."

"Yummy, yummy," I sang.

Chell shot out of the broom cupboard Nat shared
with Zebedee. She looked terrified as well as terrible.

"Rusty, she's dying. Nat's dying."

"Whajermean?"

She dragged me into the room where Nat lay, her
face a greener shade of pale, her eyes ringed with
dingy yellow. Beads of sweat stood out on her forehead, her hair was dark and streaked but when I
touched her hand it was icy.

"Don't die, Nat," wept Chell, down on her knees
by the bed.

"What's up?" I asked.

Nat moaned and turned away her face.

"Nat, Nat, what is it?"

"What is it?" she croaked. "The flip side of love,
little brother. That's what it is." Nat'd send you and
herself up if she was queueing at Heaven's gate.

"Chell, go make a cup of tea. And fill a hot water
bottle. Don't scald yourself doing it. Scram. Nat, tell
me."

"I've had an abortion and something's wrong.
That's all."

"Oh God, Nat. Why?"

She hissed back through a face that was twisted, grown old.

"I hate babies, don't I? Besides, can you see Lover Boy playing Daddy?"

"I'll fetch a doctor."

"No. Just get Soupy."

"Yeh. Yeh. Anything, Nat."

"That's what they all say."

"Hold on. I'll fix things."

I covered her up and ran to phone Soupy.

Who was there in minutes, beside the bed, holding Nat's hands. I hovered, a spare part, not knowing what to do or say, till Soupy motioned me to go, saying keep Pip out of here, and I said yes, meekly, and tiptoed away feeling pushed out, of no importance, yet guilty, women, women. Nat's suffering had been mine too. Now I was pushed out, useless.

What did it matter? I was off to see the Lynnebird. My love, my Lynnebird.

What had Nat said about love – the flip side – but then nothing like that would ever happen to Lynne. It couldn't. Lynne was different. But I walked – not ran – down the street.

And there ahead was the little chick. Standing four foot ten in high heels. I'd never seen her in high heels. And wearing make-up. Oh no. I dodged round the corner while the old computer brain sent out trillions of circuits trying to sort out what to do. At the end of it all, I came out and apologized.

"I'm sorry, I can't make it tonight," I said.

"What do you mean?"

"I can't stay." (Searched round desperately for an

excuse.) "My sister's ill and I have to get back." True and not true. There was something about Little Chick which made it difficult to lie easily.

"You mean we're not going out?"

"No, I mean, yes."

I didn't feel good at all. Her very steady, cool grey eyes looked at me as if I were some sort of slug. But it wasn't my fault.

"But I've brought all the bumf you asked for. All these."

"Great. Thanks."

"It's not great at all." The grey eyes darkened from cool to stormy. "Go jump in a lake, Patrick Gates." And throwing the leaflets all over me, she stormed off down the road. I stood there heaped in Refuse Cruise, Transport 2000, Greenpeace, Wildlife Watchers. A sneaky wind snaked round scattering Refuse Cruise . . .

"It's an offence to drop litter," a voice gloated. Mike's fuzzy ex-schoolmate, Andy Baker, stood before me in full fig. "Better gather it up like a good boy. Mm, subversive stuff is it? Be careful . . . be careful."

So I picked up Little Chick's leaflets, chasing down the road after those flurried along by the wind.

When I'd gathered them all up I walked on to the post office and posted them.

Lynne waited, stardust, moonglow. We drank coffee, then went for a long walk, telling our life stories. She told me about her mother. I told her about mine going to Greenham. But I didn't tell her about hers.

We found a fine and private place.

87

The gate at Sylvan Avenue and Lynne in my arms whispering breathily. I kept us in the shadows, in case Laura saw us.

"That was wonderful, Patrick. The most wonderful evening in my life."

The warm scent of Lynne and the cool smell of evening mingled into magic.

"It was the first time for me. You know that, don't you, Patrick?"

"Yes, I know," I murmured into the pretty pink shells, Moi, Alexander, Julius Caesar, Rockefeller, Einstein Gates. "And I'll love you for ever."

Somewhere a window banged and a cuckoo called.

But you don't hear cuckoos at this time of night, do you?

We kissed once more and she turned into the drive.

And I walked off in a state of euphoria, ecstasy, delight, rapture, in fact all of that type of emotion.

No drama. No crises. Please, you up there, don't let the fuzz be there searching for Mike, or Nat dying, don't let Chell have done anything crazy – let it be peace so that I can think about Lynne.

Seventeen Constance Place. Constance, I love you. Just let's get in and fall into the pit . . . no dramas, please.

The house slept like a baby. Nothing stirred. Mike was asleep on the downstairs sofa. He snorted suddenly, then settled. I went upstairs.

Dad came out of his bedroom. Only Dad didn't wear bra and bikini pants – Dad wasn't bony and thin and female. It was Loopy pulling on a sweater as she made her way downstairs to Mike.

Dad came to the door behind her. For once he wasn't wearing the elephant skin. Just his own. We all stared at one another in a dreadful silence.

Then we split, moving jerkily like the speeded-up figures in old films.

Chapter Thirteen

Lynne was waiting for me at the college gates. She tucked her round little soft arms into mine and kissed my cheek gently.

"Mum says I can have a party. Invite new friends, she says. She did mention you. Said you called round one evening to see me so you had a little chat. Why didn't you tell me you'd met my Mum?"

"Didn't get around to it."

"Doesn't matter. But isn't she great?" I nodded carefully. "You help me to work out who's coming."

"As long as Wally doesn't."

"Oh, poor Walter. Let him come. He keeps writing me long letters full of poetry."

"Creep."

"Well, he can still come. We'll find him a girl. What about that one you know? The amazing one. What's her name?"

"Who?" (Not Anna, please don't let it be Anna.)

"The one who rides a motor bike. You can't miss *her*, she's so beautiful. She looks like a model. You know, I was ever so jealous of her, I thought you must be crazy about her."

What a relief!

"You mean old Soups, don't you?"

"Soups?"

"Yeah. Soupy Lethbridge."

"What a funny name. Fancy being called *Soupy Lethbridge*. I shouldn't care for *that* at all."

Some passing yobs heard her and mimicked her voice and accent. I nearly splatted them. This girl made me so protective.

"Oh, you can ask ole Soups, if you like. But she's already got a boy-friend and I don't think she'd look at Wally."

"And *who* have you fancied?" she asked, snuggling up.

"Only you, Lynne."

She stopped to kiss me, and I guided her round a corner a) because I was liking it and wanting more and b) the little chick was bearing down looking like an armoured tank.

"By the way, what happened to his legs?" I asked innocently.

"Wally's legs?" She started to blush. "You were taking the mickey out of both of us," she said.

Footsteps sounded behind us.

"Thank *you* very much, Gates," said the owner of the legs himself. He was very pale, in contrast to Lynne who had blushed even more deeply. He turned to her and said:

"You might have told me yourself, Lynne, that you'd finished with me, instead of leaving me to find out from other people."

She turned her head away.

"Hey, leave it out," I shouted at him.

"As for you, I'd like to hit you so hard that you ended up in Siberia," he spat.

I laughed nonchalantly (I think that's the word).

"That'll be the day, Wally boy."

And we watched him walk away, beetroot-faced, nearly in tears. Again. Like my Dad, he's always near tears. That's because they're wet, both of them.

The spirits of gloom and doom had stopped whirling and twirling over Maison Gates and were having a sit-in on the roof. The house was falling apart with us in it. Dad never paid anything so there followed crisis after crisis as the electricity, gas, phone, water, television were threatened, followed by a frantic rush around to raise the necessary. He'd never paid Wilf Passmore for the car repairs so he couldn't have it mended when it once more juddered to a halt. The Rates Department threatened to sue him and the Inland Revenue got stroppy though what about I don't know since there didn't appear to be any income coming into Maison Gates.

He avoided me as much as I avoided him now after the terrible encounter with him and Loopy. In fact I couldn't look him in the eye. Not that I wanted to, as he sat around in the elephant skin having a weep. He and Gramps made a happy-go-lucky duo for senile decay had set in for Gramps with the loss of his Minder and his teeth got more unmanageable daily. No one took him to the Day Centre any more. He sat in the corner and chattered on and on about Mum's ingratitude, that is when he wasn't talking about having to fight Hitler before he finished. Uncle Arn, mostly paralytic, waited for his summons. Mike, jumpy, also waited for the police search he was convinced would happen at any minute.

Even Nat was at home, getting better slowly, but a changed, different Nat. She hadn't gone back to work, just sat for hours unspeaking, though occasionally she nursed Zebedee. No one phoned her.

He was happy as a bird and crawling.

Loopy had disappeared. Soupy, who dropped in every day, said she'd gone up to London to stay with their aunt. Sometimes Nat spoke to Soupy.

Pip and Chell were OK. Now I know they were *too* quiet but I wasn't interested and I'd got my own affair, my own rose glow, a shiny rainbow-coloured bubble in which I walked with and talked to and loved Lynne while every love song that was ever written was singing away just for us.

Fate couldn't harm Moi, Patrick Gates. I was magic, I was stardust. Rich, handsome and wonderful Moi.

Of course I wanted to go to Lynne's party and show her off to everybody, this luscious rich bird I'd got, great. It also felt as if I was stepping into a minefield. But I could only hope that Lynne wouldn't find out about Laura. After all, it had been only a sin that passed in the night, something that had nothing to do with the radiant relationship of Lynne and me. And no one could really hold me responsible for what happened. Laura had lain herself down with help yourself, Patrick, printed all over her and obviously knew what she was doing, being old enough to be my mother. And it would never, never, never happen again.

On Wednesday night Lynne had two lots of classes.

Later that evening as I made my way to the off-licence a car slid alongside me and stopped. The Porsche. A rabbit hypnotized by a snake, I climbed inside. For after all I had to explain that this was goodbye, that this must be the last time.

After a while it was obvious that *next* time I'd have to explain that this was goodbye, that this must be the last time. Do you know she wore *real* silk under-wear? Flame-red. Under her tracksuit.

Anyone at the Further Ed. College can get to parties if they want to as there are dozens each term from grand biggies to two or three living it up in a squat.

Lynne's had to be different. Rumours of Sylvan Avenue with money, class and endless supplies brought along everyone from those who were somebody and had been invited to those who weren't and hadn't been.

Among *them* who should turn up but Chell, wearing about fifty scarves, fifty-one bangles and her usual pipe-cleaner legs. With her was a shifty-eyed, young-old bloke with No Fixed Abode written on a tiny forehead. He made a corkscrew look straight. So that's why Chell had been quiet lately. I strode over.

"It's Glen," she began.

"Glen, Ben or Loch Lomond, you can get lost, see." I seized him by the least scrofulous bit and shook him. "She's thirteen. Now am I going to make jelly meat cat-food out of your ears and feed it to you, or am I ringing the police?"

He didn't argue. Courage wasn't his thing. As he did a runner down the drive I said to a weeping Chell:

"Now, what the heck am I going to do with you?"

A thing in black leotards and an owl mask shot up by my knees and spoke. It had a confident voice and was about the height of a tall corgi.

"I'll take care of her. She's Pip's sister. Pip is my best enemy. Nearly cleverer than me. I know you too, Patrick Gates."

"Yeah. I know you as well, Miss Martin. But thanks a lot. I'll make it worth your while." I don't know why I said that. She probably got more in pocket money per week than I would earn in a month but if she kept Chell occupied for five minutes I was grateful. I could take a look around then in peace or whatever peace I was likely to get at this do where trouble might blow in at any moment.

Mr Martin, Norman, Laura's husband and Lynne's father, was there, present in quite a lot of flesh playing the host, and he was just as I'd known he would be, tall, well-built, clothes casual but expensive, a well-spoken thug. When Lynne introduced me to him I had to swallow a hard urge to say:

"How do you do? I do very well, thank you. I've had it off with both your wife and your daughter. Lovely weather we're having."

But my blood did run cold for one moment when Laura murmured:

"Lovely boy, Patrick. You must get to know him better, Norman dear."

To that he smiled and said I must go round for a meal some time. Lynne was holding my arm very close to her. Only for a moment did I get the feeling that I was being swallowed alive by an octopus family called Martin.

Beautiful evening. Beautiful scene. Lynne beautiful in blue, Laura beautiful in silver. Everything beautiful, civilized and in good taste. Usually at college parties the parents push off. But Norman and Laura stayed and there were also lots of older people strolling about on the lawns, among the flowerbeds, in the house. Very beautiful, very civilized, very Martin.

Mind you, I was on the edgiest of edges, much as I liked the clothes, the drinks, the food. Lynne paraded me up and down. I tried to avoid Laura. I didn't want to encounter one of those knowing looks. And I didn't want to be stuck with the pair of them together, having a peculiar three-sided conversation full of hidden meanings, meaning me.

Lynne got called away and I looked round warily just in case Anna had decided to show up. Then I mooched around, drinking wine and listening to the music and yacking. And suddenly there was Little Chick in her boiler suit and wellies and lots of badges. She surveyed the scene.

"What absolute filthy bilge. And of course, you would be here, PG tips," – that was a new one on me – "you hypocrite, full of your lousy rotten . . . de – de – despicable values. This" – with a wave of the hand she dismissed it all – "would keep a family for a year in the Third World, keep a pride of lions for the rest of their lives!"

"But the Martin party doesn't make much difference. There's not very much food . . ."

"You should see what's in the kitchen."

"I haven't been poking around in the kitchen, unlike you . . ."

"I had to. The cat had hurt its foot and I went in there to sort it out. Don't try to get me away from the point. All that alcohol."

"Smashing. I'll get you some."

"No thanks. I'm going. I just wanted to tell you off and I've done that now. Besides, I've work to do."

"Don't be like that. I couldn't help . . ."

"Yes, you could. You were after her" – she indicated Lynne with a jerk of the head – "all the time, and just using me."

"I didn't use you much," I cried, hurt. "Look, be friends."

"Never. You've ruined men for me, P. Gates. You know what you are . . ."

96

"I've got a fair idea."

"You're a – a – a shit."

And off she stomped down the drive on poggy legs. Sometimes I think I need a course on "How To Win Friends and Influence People". But so what? Who cared about Little Chick (except Little Chick) now re-christened Little Virago? Where had Lynne got to?

She was weaving her way towards me, taking ages, because the idiot brigade kept stopping her for no good reason. Why didn't she tell them all to get lost? Suddenly I felt fed up. The band was revolting, no talent at all, and the whole place was full of people I hated the sight of. I'd much rather have been alone with Lynne than watching her with some balding geezer old enough to be her grandad. Knocking back two glasses of wine (that just happened to be handy) I strode after her, grasped her masterfully (women like that) and hauled her into the shrubbery.

Slap went her hand on my face. Ouch.

"What's that about?"

"Don't you dare maul me. Especially here. What would Mummy think?"

I just stopped myself saying that Mummy'd probably love it.

"Sorry, Lynne. You're so beautiful, you see. It drove me mad with desire. It won't happen again." (You cow.) "I promise."

"OK, my love. Oh, it's just that. Well, you know. I can't HERE. I'll make it up to you later."

I managed to press her closely to me before she scrambled out of the (I think) laurel bush.

"I'll hold you to that."

"Now, I must go and speak to Uncle Teddy. He's

my godfather and he's come down specially to see me. Come and meet him. He's over there."

I took one look at Uncle Teddy and thought no. Something about Uncle Teddy's smooth hair and roving eyes gave me the feeling we would never be soul-mates.

"I'll wait here, darling. Don't be long. Then we'll push off on our own."

She smiled vaguely and hurried, yes, hurried away from Moi. I stood moodily by the laurel bush, wondering if I'd bother to go inside. Was enjoyment all it was cracked up to be? I wasn't having much of a time. And I didn't like what Lynne was wearing – she looked, I dunno, different. I supposed I might as well wander inside and hang about. Something was bound to turn up. More time passed. I realized I was bored and drank some more wine.

And there, of course, was Laura. Conversation wasn't really one of our things these days. I didn't say a word as she pulled me through the shrubbery into an orchard. Fruit hung about everywhere as I followed her to what looked like a sprawled carpet of leaves. To my surprise grapes hung there as well. Inside the carpet was a small shed full of tools and, naturally, a blanket.

"*Lady Chatterley's Lover*. I must read it some time," I thought as we settled on it. After which I didn't think about anything at all.

"I must get back to my guests," Laura said, brushing herself down and fixing on some lipstick in the gloom. "Wait for three minutes. Then come."

Chewed round the edges, I waited, then nervously emerged. All was quiet. I made my way back to the laurel bush and posted myself there, trying to look as if I'd never left it. I felt very tired. Another drink would help. I looked around for one.

"Hoy," said a voice behind me, a voice I knew. Like a fool I turned, for it was only Wally. And he hit me, crack, hard on the face right where Lynne had hit me. It hurt, bringing tears to my eyes. How could you, Wally? After all these days. He was running away from me, very fast. I started to follow – more in sorrow than in anger – and fell over something small crawling out of the undergrowth wearing an owl mask. I staggered upright. It was the mocking-bird sister. Chell lurked behind.

"That'll be fifteen quid," said the mocking bird, through the mask.

"What?" I wasn't hearing properly. She took off the mask and grinned. No Lynne, this one. More like a frog.

"A fiver for looking after her. You'll have to take her home now. Dead boring, isn't she? Then ten not to tell Lynne."

"Tell Lynne what?"

"About you and Mum, 'course. Fifteen quid."

"I haven't got fifteen quid! And if I had I wouldn't give it to you. It's blackmail!"

"So? I'll give you till Monday. If not I'll tell Lynne. In fact make it twenty. Then I won't tell Dad, about you and them both."

"You're a monster!"

"Yes. And I know what you are."

"What?" I asked before I could stop myself.

"Stupid. Till Monday. Take her home. Bye, Chell."

And it vanished back to wherever it belonged, brrrhh!

I stood dazed. This evening was spinning me out of control. Part of me wanted to run and hide. But –

"Oh, there you are, darling," cried Lynne, hurrying over. "Who's this?"

"It's my little sister. I'd better take her home. She shouldn't be here."

"Oh, don't be stuffy. Let's all go inside and dance. Come on. The music's great. You like discos, don't you?"

"Yes," said Chell, brightening.

"You can dance with us. All three of us. Come on, Patrick."

"Thank you. All I ever wanted was to dance with Chell," but they were already dragging me indoors, where the music was blowing wild.

"Your friend never turned up," bellowed Lynne as we hopped around.

"Which friend?"

"The glamorous one. Soups or something. I wanted her for Wally."

"Er."

"He came, you know. He was ever so sweet."

"What? I can't hear."

"He – was – ever – so – sweet. Said – he – forgave – me."

"Oh, did he?"

"What did you say?"

"Nothing."

"What have you done to your poor face?"

"Your sweet Wally."

"What did you say?"

"Never mind."

The music stopped abruptly and Soupy in her black leathers strode in. Straight for me. Lynne began to speak to her but Soupy wasn't listening.

"Sorry. I can't stop. There's trouble at home,

100

Gatesy. Come on. Get on my bike and we'll go."

"What is it?"

"I'll fill you in later."

"I've got Chell."

"OK. I'll take her. And you come as fast as you can. It's urgent. Bye, Lynne. Sorry."

She'd gone and Chell with her.

"I can only say sorry, Lynne."

"She's bossy. Do you have to go? The evening's just warming up."

"I think I must."

"I'll come to the gate with you. What a ghastly family you've got. Mum at Greenham, that awful kid sister, crisis after crisis. Your Mum's fault, I suppose. Never mind, I'll look after you. I'll be your family."

I wasn't as pleased with that as I should have been. Me saying how awful they were was one thing, someone else, even Lynne, doing so, another. I pressed her hand back against the gate and kissed her for a long time to take away not liking her much just then.

Something pulled me off her. I turned round.

"Well, well. If it isn't the two-timing lover boy?" A voice from behind me brought me sharply back to reality. "Just how many girl-friends have you got? Not that it matters, because after we finish with you the Bride of Frankenstein wouldn't fancy you."

"Lynne, run," I just managed to shout.

But she didn't. She was watching and listening.

Behind me were two large wide blokes, neither of whom I had encountered before but with somehow vaguely familiar features.

"What do you want? I don't even know you."

"But we know you, Casanova. Shall we introduce ourselves? I'm Jim and this is Bert and we happen to be related to your ex-girl-friend Anna." Nice to be introduced, I thought.

"So what? We've split up. Can't she accept it gracefully?"

"What do you mean, so what? She's pregnant, you bastard."

A choked cry sounded behind, followed by the sound of running feet, but I couldn't see what was happening to Lynne for as this news seized me up, they caught up with me. Bert grabbed me from behind and Jim started punching me in the face. Desperately I kicked out and connected with Jim's shin, which made him howl, and I jabbed Bert in his midriff, which had little effect and didn't cause him to relinquish his grip. Why hadn't I taken up self-defence? I bent my head lower to try to avoid Jim's punches and suddenly smashed the back of my head into Bert's face. That made him let go.

But Jim kicked me in the groin and I collapsed. The now recovered Bert kicked me in the ribs as I lay in agony, and hissed:

"When Anna next wants to see you, you'd better be there. If you're not, you'll have hell to pay."

From the pavement I watched them walking away, sick and sore and swollen. Lynne had disappeared. After about ten minutes I got up and hobbled down the road.

What about Lynne? What about my sex life? Was this the end?

Painfully home. Oh, Constance Place – why did I ever grind on about you? You were all I wanted, Constance Place, sanctuary, somewhere to lay my head. Back at Maison Gates. Oh, Anna.

Oh, Lynne. Oh, me! Oh, what a mess.

"You took your time," grumbled Soupy, opening the door. I couldn't get the key in the lock. Something to do with my right eye closing up rapidly.

"Oh, my God. Who got you? Sit there. Stay." As if I was a dog. But I wasn't going anywhere.

Up on the roof the dooms clattered and banged happily. Seventeen Constance Place was great. Nat sat weeping. Loopy was kneeling beside my father, lying on the sofa white as death. A sinister bucket and many towels were heaped up beside him.

"What happened?" I muttered through the mushy remains of my mouth.

"Overdose. After the police took Mike. They found his supply."

A feeble flicker of curiosity stirred behind the urge to lie down and die too.

"Where?"

"In the car."

"Oh. Is he all right? Dad, I mean. Ouch, that hurt, Soups."

"Shut up. Yeah. Loopy was here and she made him sick."

I tried to smile and couldn't. She always makes people sick. But I couldn't say it.

"But that's nothing," went on Soupy. "Hurry up and recover, Squeaky. You and I are up, up and away as soon as you're up to it."

"What are you talking about?"

"Pip's run away. She's left a note, thank goodness. She's gone to find your Mum," – and as if a button had been pressed –

"I want my Mum," Nat cried, weeping, weeping, weeping as if she'd never stop.

Chapter Fourteen

"You see, in a strange sort of way, I'm happy," Mum said.

She smiled at me and stirred the wood fire. It was cold in the early morning but at least it wasn't raining. I sat on a box wrapped in an old blanket, drinking a sweet smoky cup of tea with great care for it hurt. We were in a clearing under the trees, sheltered by a large polythene sheet draped above us over and through the branches, making a kind of cave filled with boxes, bags, books, pans, blankets, bundles. Nearby three more polythene sheets were draped over branches to make tents, benders Mum had called them. Pip was asleep in one. Soupy had gone walkabout to see people and hand out some bits and pieces, paperbacks, grub and ciggies. Mum sat on an ancient chair.

"I'll get you something to eat," she said. "They haven't raided us lately so we've got some."

"Raided?" I asked stupidly. I didn't feel too good.

"The bailiffs come and take everything. Except what you can hang on to. It's not nice. But it means you get your priorities right."

"Besides," she went on, "we haven't been done as much as the others. Perhaps because we're one of the little gates."

"Gates?"

"There are several. Greenham's big, y'know. Nine

miles round, and there are several gates in that nine miles opening on to the Common. That's where the wimmin live, have their camps. At the gates. They're called after colours. Blue, Green, Indigo, Yellow, Orange. It all started at the Main Gate. The first protest against the missiles. The Wimmin's protest. 1981 it began. "Women for Life on Earth" came to Greenham. Not long after the Camps became women only."

I didn't know what to say.

Then she looked round and said:

"I like it here. My garden's coming on nicely. Look."

There was a small square edged round with stones, with little, rather tatty flowers growing in it, like the gardens we made as kids that never lasted the summer. A cat jumped on to her lap and bedded down.

"We've got a lot of cats. They seem to like it here. You'll have to get down, Pussy Cat. Patrick'll need feeding."

My mother sat there perfectly happy, talking away as if she were at her country cottage. What right had she to be totally serene? I'd got to get things clear to her, though it looked to me as if she was completely round the twist.

"I don't want any food. I feel rough."

"Yes, you look terrible, lad."

She didn't sound as if she cared.

"Mum, you must listen to me. It's really grim at home. You must come and sort things out."

Which disaster should I tell her about first?

"Dad took an overdose of aspirin."

"Again? He always did when things got difficult.

But not a proper one. He always counted carefully. I remember when Mike was born . . ."

"MUM! Listen. Mike. He might go to prison."

"That might be the best thing. To cure him, I mean."

I couldn't believe my ears. What had happened to the ever-loving doormat?

"Nat, Nat . . . she's had an abortion."

"I often thought I should've done that when Pip was on the way. Five was too much for me. But who would be without Pip? She's worth the rest put together. Though you could be worse, I suppose."

"Mum." I felt sick. "I'm horrible. I can't tell you what I've been doing . . ." Oh, it was hopeless.

"Mm. Screwing, you mean. It'll sort out. You'll come all right in the end."

"I'm just a shit. Like people say. I can't stand me. Yuk. I couldn't even pass my driving test which I wanted to do mainly so I could come and see you."

There was a noise. Someone was stirring in one of the benders.

"They won't mind me being here, will they? Being a bloke and all that?"

"No, we don't mind. Lots of men visit us and show support."

I felt bewildered, lost in something I didn't understand.

"Why are you here? What's it all about?"

She was silent. I had almost dropped off in front of the fire, and came to with a start. She stirred, pushed the cat off her lap and put some more wood on the fire. She crouched beside it, looking up at me.

At last she stood up.

"Are you all right?"

"Yeah, I think so. Just tired, that's all."

"Your right eye's closed up. I'll get you something for it. Here."

I held the wet rag to my throbbing eye. Oh Lord, I felt awful. All I wanted to do was lie down and sleep, sleep. What was Mum doing to me? To us?

"Come with me, Patrick. I want to show you."

We walked up to the high wire fence, which seemed totally unreal, the high wire fence, tied with rags, some just blowing in the breeze, some woven into webs. Oh yes, the webs. I remembered Pip's poem. Where we stood outside the fence, grew trees and plants. The cats roamed. It was untidy but green and alive. On the other side of the fence a soldier in full uniform stood beside a ramshackle hut. How did he feel? In there with the Americans, keeping our people out. I didn't want him to see me. I should've dressed in drag, I thought. It was bleak and bare on the other side of the fence, tarmac, army vehicles, dark rectangular huts, the sinister bunkers where lay –

"The machines of death," said Mum. "Just there. Before us. Here on the outside of the wire is life, inside there is death. The world is mad, Patrick."

We walked on together, round the wire. I'm at the famous Greenham Common, I thought. We went on further along the rutted path to the next Gate where Mum thought we might catch up with Soupy and I could meet some of the girls . . . she smiled . . .

For once in my life I didn't want to meet some of the girls . . .

I felt completely out of my depth in something I didn't understand. Mum seemed to be herself yet more so, as if she'd grown stronger and more sure. Yet hadn't she always been the strongest force in

Seventeen, Constance Place, in fact in Constance Place itself?

Which was all the more reason for not leaving us all to stew so miserably in our own juice. I felt as if I were five years old again and had been told to tidy my own things, get my shoelaces tied, face washed, teeth cleaned, hair tidied and left to get on with it on my own.

On the other side of the wire army vehicles drove backwards and forwards, playing Chinese chequers. Soldiers slithered through the grass on their bellies. A siren sounded.

"They keep them busy," said Mum.

We continued to walk for a long time. The Common was big, the rough heath land and scrubby trees stretched on for miles. I hadn't realized it would be so big. Mum talked as if . . . Mum talked on as if she couldn't stop. Talking notebook to herself as much as me.

"It's not the Russians, the Americans, the loony brigade pressing the button in error, the other countries catching up with their nukes. It's become a fight against the weapons themselves. They are the enemy. It's a race between the nukes and us. That's the arms race. You understand, Rusty?"

"Sort of."

I could hear her voice against the trees.

"For the planet. For the children and the animals. Even for Constance Place." I came to. She was in my world again.

"But you're not helping Constance Place. It doesn't have to be *you* here. You've got other things to do where you're important. What you do here makes no difference."

She didn't reply.

"Why only women here?"

But it was no use. I'd gone beyond. I made it to one of the bender things, where they covered me up. How could Moi be so tired and ache so much?

Bang. Where am I? What the hell? What's happening? Let me out of here! Shouts, bangs, shrieks, screams, noise all about me, the air throbbing, the ground shaking. I must get out of here. Christ, I'm smothering! Is this it? I'm being attacked, dragged, smothered, bumped, kicked, I must be dying – oh, oh HELL!!! I'm suffocating! Oh, pain, oh, pain.

"Mum – get me out of here."

"There's someone under here!" The shouts are right above me now.

"It's a bloke. What's he doing here?"

The bailiffs had arrived.

It was a fortnight before we got home, a muddled fortnight in which I had concussion and flu while friends of Soupy – that girl has friends all over the place – looked after me and Pip, and Mum was picked up and questioned.

During that fortnight something happened. A Russian reactor blew up in a place we'd never heard of. A radioactive cloud spread over Europe.

The name of the place was Chernobyl.

Epilogue

For Sale by *Force* read the post stuck outside Seventeen, Constance Place. Mum, Pip and Moi stood staring at it several days later. What a terrible name for an Estate Agent to have, shot into my mind and out again. The front door was freshly painted green and a large terracotta pot stood outside it, overflowing with flowers. Constance was transformed and sparkling, with white painted sills and windows shining. The door was locked. The sunshine lit up the newly decorated hall as we let ourselves in.

It didn't feel like Constance Place. But then I didn't feel much like Patrick Gates, Moi. My left foot was in a plaster, my eye was rainbow-coloured and my mind in a whirl.

Over the past weeks I'd tried to think things through as they say. Me and Moi had had quite a few arguments, with neither of us winning. I didn't really know what to do about anything at all, though I'd managed to borrow twenty quid from Soupy for the mocking bird blackmailer. I didn't tell Soupy what for and she didn't ask, but then she wouldn't.

Pip had rushed away upstairs immediately to check and review her possessions. Mum was making tea in the newly immaculate kitchen when the phone rang. I hobbled to answer it.

"Is that you, Patrick? It's your Aunt Edna."

"I'll get Mum for you."

"No, you'll do. Just want you to know that Arnold and Gramps are safely with me. Bessie will be pleased to hear that they've both settled down really well. I found them in very poor shape. I was surprised. Tell Bessie I'll be in touch. She'll stay at home now, of course. Though it's a bit late closing the stable door after the horse has bolted . . ."

"What?"

"You'll soon find out. She's asked for it, I think."

"Aunt Edna, what . . . ?"

But she'd put down the phone. I told Mum, "I've got this feeling something strange is going on."

"You're quick," she replied.

I felt very uneasy. Hindered by this ankle, I couldn't run very fast if Anna's mob set on me. I wished I'd stayed in Newbury.

"Look, sit down and drink your tea. Thank heaven for a comfortable chair. I wonder where everybody is? But someone will turn up to let us know. Let's have a rest before it all starts happening."

It soon began. Soupy appeared, dressed up in a blouse and suit and high-heeled shoes, looking like a pure gold wonder.

"Thought I'd drop in," she said. "I'm off up to London. Interview for a new job. But I hoped you'd be here. I've got things to tell you and I didn't want it to be a shock. It's not easy. Sorry. But someone has to so I suppose it'll be me."

She pulled off her gloves – gloves! – and sat down.

"Liz," she began to my Mum.

"Liz?" I butted in.

"I hate the name Bessie," Mum said. "I changed it some time ago but the family didn't notice."

"It's difficult for me, Liz. Oh well, here goes.

Ronnie," (my Dad, what about my Dad?) "Ronnie's moved in with Loopy. They say they're very happy. In a flat – I've got the address for you, and Chell's with them. She's fine. Pip can go there too if she wants."

Mum sat silent, her face without expression.

"And Mike? What about him?" I croaked at last.

"He's undergoing a cure. They're quite optimistic about it, apparently. I've got his address, too. Oh Liz, don't mind about it."

"No, no, I shan't. I haven't loved him for a long time, or liked him, even though it takes a lot of getting used to. I'll be all right." But she still looked dazed.

"I mind," cried Pip from the doorway. "I want to be with Mum and Rusty, not Dad and Chell."

"Natalie?" asked Mum.

"She's fine. She's staying with me at present. She packed in that job and is learning to look after Zebedee, so that he'll recognize her, she says. She's done most of the work here. Ronnie wants to sell it, which is why the sale notice is outside, but Nat thinks it could be made into two flats. She'd stay with Zebedee, find someone to look after him when she gets a new job, and Pip and Patrick could stay here and you come at week-ends. If you think it could work, she'll talk Ronnie into not selling after all."

"I think I'll make another cup of tea while I get my breath back," said Mum.

Soupy pulled on the gloves.

"I must go."

"I'll come to the door with you. That's about my limit."

"It'll soon mend."

We stood together in the hall. I was just about to ask about Anna when she said, grinning:

"I've got some more news as well. Everything's been happening here."

"What?"

"Walter Byack's engaged to Anna."

"NO!!!"

"Oh yes."

The sun flooded Constance Place. I'd have danced the tango if I could have danced a tango. Anna engaged! I could bear to go on living. A thought struck me. Did he know? And would it be – mine? And, good old Wally. My friend to the end.

"There's something else," went on Soupy. "The Martins have gone, disappeared, done a moonlight flit. Rumours are rife, y'know. Fraud, embezzlement. Mum ran off with his brother, Teddy or something. Poor Lynne. She wasn't a bad kid." She peered closely at me. "Upset?"

"Me? No. Found I didn't like her much. Nor her sister . . . brrh."

I could pay back the twenty pounds! Amazing. Overnight things had changed. I thought I was the one who'd have to make things different but I could only hang on as everything else and everybody else moved on ahead of me. Only Soupy remained constant. Beautiful, strong Soupy, always there.

"See you, Squeaky," she said, kissing me gently on a non-bruised bit. "Take care."

"Don't go. Don't ever leave, Soups."

"I have to. And if they offer me this job I'll take it. Now don't get dramatic. I'll be back. Not too many girls, Squeaky – not all at once."

"How could I? It's you I love. Not the others. I've always been crazy about you. Be my girl, Soups."

"Nah." She laughed again. But not unkindly. "Not me. I'd never do. Try Eunice Grant."

"Eunice Grant?"

"A little girl. Into causes. She's crazy about you. Now I really must go. Bye, Squeaky. Take care."

She walked away from me whistling, on her ten-foot-long legs, turning to wave as she reached the corner on her way to London, to the world, to the top, leaving us all behind.

"Patrick," called out Mum. "Let's sort things out. I'd like to go back to Greenham as soon as possible. There's lots to do."

You're telling me, I thought, as I hobbled back inside Seventeen Constance Place.

Mum said she hoped Chernobyl would change everything. But it didn't. I didn't think it would since people are people. So she's going to continue her fight for peace. (I always knew it was a loony bin planet, fancy fighting for peace.) The rest of us will just rub along surviving, I suppose. I might even try a bit harder at not being a shit. And maybe . . . Mum could be right.

The door bell rang. I hobbled back again and opened it. A girl stood there. She had black hair, eyes like dark pools, and a figure with more ins and outs than the coast of Scotland.

I put on my best grin, the one that fetched Tracey Brewer all those years ago.

"Hello," she said. "Is this house for sale? Do I have to make an appointment to see it?"

"Oh yes . . . no. Come in," I answered. "Let me introduce myself. My name is Patrick Gates, entrepreneur, future millionaire, nineteen years old," (which was a lie) . . .

Author's Footnote

All the time that Patrick Gates was pursuing his merry path through the local female population, it was slowly dawning on us that the twentieth century's answer to the Black Death was here to stay. And that it wasn't just a minority's problem.

Would the idea of AIDS change Patrick Gates, I wondered? *Could* it change Patrick Gates? Would he stick to one partner? Could he?

At present he's seen around with Eunice Grant, the Little Chick. And he's working hard, learning to be a reporter on Uncle Arnold's newspaper.

Will a job and Little Chick be enough for Gatesy?